Man in the Cellar

stories by
JULIA O'FAOLAIN

FABER AND FABER
3 Queen Square
London

First published in 1974
by Faber and Faber Limited
3 Queen Square London WC1
Printed in Great Britain by
Latimer Trend & Company Ltd Plymouth
All rights reserved

ISBN 0 571 10515 7

Contents

ACKNOWLEDGEMENTS

Some of these stories have already appeared in the following: *Winters' Tales, London Magazine, Critic, Cosmopolitan, Mademoiselle.*

Man in the Cellar

Signora,

Yes: "Signora"!

You will see why we must become more formal. I have a message for you. Take it seriously. IT IS NOT A JOKE.

Carlo (yours and mine) is at this moment chained to a bedstead in the lower cellar of our house. He can only move about half a metre. His shouts cannot be heard outside the house and nobody can get into it. The doors and shutters are locked. The keys are in a bucket at the bottom of the backyard well. All you have to do when you get there is turn the crank and pull it up. Inside, on a key-ring, are the keys to the front and cellar doors and a smaller one for the padlocks which fasten Carlo's chains.

Relax, Signora. His discomfort is minor. Think of Bangladesh.

He has food and water for several days. He has air, electric light, warmth and a slop bucket within reach. Unless a fire breaks out—and why should it?—he is safe. It is up to you to release him. You can give him life a second time.

I can't.

It was I who chained him up—to his astonishment and, I may fairly say, frenzy. If I let him loose now, there is a real danger that he might kill me before he comes to his senses. You know what his temper is like. You never taught him to control it. This dilemma has been growing more acute over the last few weeks—I have held him prisoner for a month—and the only solution I can see is for me to send you this letter and leave. Obviously, I do not expect to return and shall tell neither you nor Carlo where I am going.

The following points should be clarified at once:

1. Carlo's employers and colleagues think he has resigned from his job. I sent them a letter to that effect a month ago. I forged his signature.

2. I have given it out locally that he is in England where my stepfather has offered him a job and where I expect to join him shortly.

3. *For Carlo's sake*, try not to blab the truth about at once. Give him a chance to think up some cover story to save his face. Also: don't bring anyone else with you when you go to release him. Do you want him to be a laughing-stock?

4. I regret the mess in which our marriage is ending, and I shall do everything I can to make it easy for Carlo to get an annulment. A divorce would be good enough for me but I know it wouldn't suit you and may not Carlo. His experience with me may send him quailing back to the ways of Holy Mother Church: Mum's religion. He may want a Mum-picked, virginal bride next time and girls like that want a church wedding. I have written a page of a longer letter which I intend to leave addressed to you in my bedroom-desk—stating that I never intended our marriage to be permanent, that I entered on it in bad faith and never intended having children by Carlo. I should think any canon lawyer would find all he needed here to invalidate the bond—especially the way they're handing out annulments these days. You see: I didn't entirely waste my time at those churchy dinner-parties of yours where your eminent friend, Count C., used to hold forth so interminably. I recall, by the way, with some joyless amusement, the occasion when I asked him wouldn't it be easy to fake the conditions required for an annulment and *you* cut in with: "But, Una dear, what would be the point? One cannot lie to God." I do not say that my page x is all lies but *if it were* would you object to my lying to God on Carlo's behalf? Or might you not feel that the lie of a lapsed Protestant was justified by its end? Luckily, you don't have to reply!

5. I shall stay on with Carlo for twelve hours after posting this. Posts between Volterra and Florence being what they are, I daren't stay longer. This means that, at best, he will have been alone only an hour or so when this reaches you and, at worst,

a day. It shouldn't take you more than two hours to drive here.

By the way: did you notice anything odd about the letters you got from Carlo while you were in Austria? I wrote them.

Never mind, Signora, I'm on my way.

I hope you are too. Get into your car or taxi. Yes: take a taxi. You are distraught and we can't afford an accident at this point —which is why I'm registering this. It tells you all you need to know for now. You will find a fuller explanation of what happened in the letter in my bedroom-desk drawer. That took me some days to write. It is an apologetic (sic), not as formal as I would, in retrospect, have liked, but I have no time to re-write it. Now that I am finally leaving, I regret the bitterness— the insolence—of its tone. But what do I not regret? And what use is regret? Embittered relationships pollute lives. Better dissolve them and recycle the elements. I am recycling myself. I'm orbiting off. Good-bye, Signora Crispi,

(signature) Una

The following pages, sealed in a large foolscap-size envelope addressed to Signora Francesca Crispi did not, as the narrative will show, ever reach her.

When I think of the satisfaction this letter will give you, I have to stop myself tearing it up. You, I have to remind myself, are a minor figure in all this and your reactions do not matter one way or the other. Besides, I *want* to write everything out once, sequentially—then I will probably never think of it again. I will manage to muffle as much of it as possible in that private blanket of oblivion that I can feel, almost *see* in my brain sometimes. I pull it down like a soft, hairy, comforting screen. It is brown, woolly (maybe a memory of a pram-rug in my infancy?), and I summon it when I want to blot out some nasty memory. It always works. One can only use it when one intends getting right away from reminders or wit-nesses to the event to be blotted out: which is what I am doing. I've done it before. It is surprisingly easy to do when you live in big cities. I can see your disapproval, poor provincial lady! You twitch and tut-tut and nod and shake your head and start in on your repertoire of gesture—like an animal. Half the words

you use are meaningless. I used to count them at meals sometimes, the number of meaningless words you used: baby-talk,
grunt-words, expletives. Even *I* speak better Italian than you
do most of the time, Signora! If you were forbidden to say
uffa, tsts, bah, beh, ma, macchè, magari, thth (tongue wetly parting
company with pre-dental palate), *toh, totò, caca, pipi, poppò,
moh, già, eh, oh, ah, eeh* and a few more, you would be at a total
loss. You might even lose your reason, like animals whose
familiar environment has been abruptly changed for some
scientific experiment. I used to imagine I was the scientist
doing it to you. It was one of my favourite fantasies: blot *uffa
tsts, bah*, etc. out of Signora Crispi's mind and observe
results. Subject shows signs of incipient paranoia. Begins to
cluck. Prevent clucking. Subject whimpers. Prevent whimper-
ing. Subject reveals withdrawal symptoms, reverts to animal pos-
ture, crawls on all fours, barking. Memo: prevent this. Subject
stupefied in trance or fit or otherwise. I played this scenario
in my head through many a lunch. Tell me where is fancy bred?
In frustration, rage or sheer bloody boredom.

Maybe I should have had some sisterly pity for *your* frustra-
tions? Even proverbs know that *"chi dice 'ma,' core contento non
ha!"* But I was too unhappy myself to worry about you.

Sudden doubt: could it be that you truly *are* paranoiac—I've
wondered on occasion—that you might not release poor Carlo
but keep him tied by the legs, the way you had him as a baby?
That I've given him back to you just as you always wanted
him: dependent. You can clean up his *caca*, give him *totò*, be
la mammina again to your somewhat oversize *pezzetino, donnino,
piccino-picciò*? God, how I hate baby-talk. I take this seriously.
It is not inconceivable. I think I'd better send a telegram from
Milan to the local police chief, warning him to check on you.
I owe it to Carlo. Three days after my first letter reaches you,
the telegram will be sent. And another to the family doctor.
So watch it, lady.

Facts: I want to tell you the facts. In sequence. I despair of
explaining *why* I did what I did—though, oddly, I feel you
may understand. Power-games are well known to you, Signora
Crispi. *How* I did it will be more easily narrated.

First: my need for equipment, i.e. weapons. Carlo, as you know, is a big man for an Italian and in good shape. When we fight, he wins: history of the sex-war. I wonder did you ever fight his father? Physically, I mean? *Macchè!* I see you sniff, purse your lips, half shrug, turn away. *Tsts!* A woman has her own weapons. A true woman uses tact, charm, humour, patience. Translate: guile, pussy and a readiness to let herself be humiliated. Right? Right. I've used them all. I've enjoyed them. Some sick pleasures can be touched off by nausea. In Carlo too. Your son, Signora, is not quite the clean-cut Mamma's boy you sometimes like to think.

The last few sentences may not mean much to you. That's just too bad. I have no time to bridge the culture divide *and* the generation gap. It would take more than Caesar and his minions to build a bridge like that. I was coming to the question of equipment, tools, weapons in the most simple sense —metaphor will get us nowhere. To spell it out: Carlo used to knock me about.

Try to understand this: I had never known people hit each other until Carlo did it to me. My parents never hit me, much less each other. It would not have occurred to them to do so. It was not part of my experience. It was something one saw happen in films or read about. It happened, one knew, in the more old-fashioned boys' schools: a purely masculine, rather retrograde practice which should, and soon would, be abolished like hanging and the birch. If Carlo had threatened me with a chastity belt or infibulation, I could have hardly been more outraged and determined to resist, whatever the risks—and there were risks.

You've seen me with a black eye. It wasn't the only one I got. I had to go to a doctor with a dislocated neck, and again with my nose. The inside is all twisted up even though the line of my profile is unchanged—which is lucky since I intend to peddle my wares on new markets. (Am I annoying you?) Anyway, these rows didn't always end in bed. Sometimes, as the front door banged, I was left alone and seething with the bitterness of the impotent. Oh yes, I have hated Carlo. Remember we had practically no money. That miserable job your cousin got him with the safe pension at the end was—but I must keep to the point. We were going through a bad time, fighting maybe once a day and although I was terrified of being disfigured, I put my pride in never backing down. Verbally, I am a champion. I can humiliate, ridicule, provoke, dose my effects, deviate things towards a little sado/masochistic romp or escalate to what sounds like a final rupture—would *be* a final rupture if we weren't living in Volterra and, as often as not, without the fare to Florence in our communal kitty. I suppose I half enjoyed those rows. I had nothing else to do. Volterra is not a jumping place. The cinemas seemed to show a sequence of slapstick films by Ciccio and Ingrassia—a *purely* Italian taste, may I say—or else those panoramic wet-dreamers' fantasies designed for Near-Eastern markets. They bored me. I was bored. I had intended doing some designs for shirt fabrics and sending them back to London where an old art-school mate was to try and flog them for me, but somehow I did very few during our year in Volterra and what I did didn't get sold.

I blamed Carlo. The letters from London were kind but I could tell my old friend thought my stuff lousy and that it was living in Italy and being spoilt and lazy that was the trouble. This bothered me. You see I *had* been good. I had been one of the few people who actually got work while still at art school. Nobody doubted but that I would make out. The scholarship to Rome—won in the teeth of several talented men—was supposed to have set me on the high road to success. It turned out to be a high road to Carlo and an existence just a shade more stimulating than a battery hen's.

Oh, you tried to help! You used to invite me to Florence and "occupy" me with visits to dressmakers and hen parties. God, the grotesquerie of those! The quintessential vacancy of the talk! Its sediment is stuck in my brain: kernels of dehydrated, interchangeable chat. Just mix and stir: "Darling/super/oh/ genuine/real/pure Austrian loden/English tweed/morals/mohair /porn. . . . My little-woman-who-knits. . . . My little antique dealer. . . ." (You had nothing but dwarves at your service!) "Have another cup of. . . . What a lovely cup. . . . Yes, from

Capodimonte. My aunt left me a set of cups, but when the charwoman broke a cup and I tried to replace it, they said, 'Signora, that cup.' . . ." Uuugh! Eeeegh!

I used to imagine someone had done a lobotomy on me. It was a nightmare I kept getting: my brain had been furtively removed. When I woke up I was never really reassured. I'd hear myself sounding like *you*. When I was still trying to perfect my Italian I used to copy your intonations and later began to feel I'd sucked in your mental patterns as well. "*Si, diamine*," I'd hear me say, "I always wear pure silk next to my skin: so much cooler and a natural fabric. . . ." Actually, when you got intellectual, you were worse. It could be so embarrassing when you sounded off on ecology that sometimes I'd interrupt to ask how to make a "true" lentil *purée* and get you back to what you understood. You never minded. Lentil *purée* was closer to your real interests. "*Pian, pianino*," you'd recommend, "that's the whole of it. Never let them boil up. *Pian, pianino*. Slow but sure! *Chi va piano va sano e va lontano!* Remember that, Una!" Once I dreamed I was making lentil *purée*. All night, endlessly, repetitively, I kept stirring the brown, manure-like slop, the smooth, cosy *caca*. *Pian, pianino!* Stir, stir. When I woke up I had a crying fit.

"I've lost my mind," I told Carlo. "I'm turning into a cow like your mother!"

"Must you be rude about my mother?"

"I'm not rude. *She* thinks women are cows. She's quite happy to be a cow!" I said. "She's always saying it. 'Pick women and oxen from your native district,' is her number one favourite saw. *Donne e buoi dai paesi tuoi*. Do you think", I screamed, "that that's polite to *me*?"

"She's very patient," said Carlo. "She's a saint. You do everything you can to embarrass her with her friends. What would it cost you to conform a bit?"

"A saint? Shit!"

"Words like that . . ."

"Shit, shit, shit!" I roared so the neighbours would hear.

Carlo went to have his breakfast alone in a café.

That was the day I bought the shackles from the old-iron man, the *ferraiuolo* who used to pass by once a month with an old cart drawn by a mule.

I wonder can I make you understand? Am I mad to try? How could you see my reality with my eyes? But I want you to. I want to make you. Once. Even if only while you read this. Then you will reject it, feel contaminated and try desperately to wash off the memory and flush it out with talk, exclaiming and wringing your hands.

The *ferraiuolo* is a dry old man whom I like. He goes down our street at regular intervals, shouting his cry, buying and selling old iron—buying mostly or even cadging. He scarcely expects to *sell* any in our middle-class district. Sometimes, though, he has a few hooks for hanging flowerpots from balconies or some other appurtenance of bourgeois living: an old lantern, some piece of wrought iron he hopes might please our knowing eye. I often give him coffee. This is not the done thing. You disapprove. You've told me so. The neighbours find it odd. Oh all your forebodings are being confirmed! I can see your smug, martyred look as you read this.

I had been fantasizing a lot over the previous months: daydreaming. My scenarios were banal. In one, a design of mine won a prize and led to my getting a job in London which was so well paid that Carlo threw his up and followed me. This made me the breadwinner and very soon he began to feel diminished. This was the climax of the dream which would then taper off in a *largo maestoso* with *me* comforting *him*. A more satisfying scenario dealt with our fights but reversed their pattern. In the dream I won. Usually, I turned out to have been taking secret karate lessons and one day when he was being especially odious I would suddenly throw him over my shoulder. It was an orgasmic dream and had to be used sparingly. I only indulged in it when I was feeling particularly humiliated. It was a great pick-me-up. After a few good dream kicks or karate throws, I felt sorry for Carlo and rather tender towards him. When the real Carlo came home, he was astonished to find me changed from a resentful termagant into quite an amiable wife. I think he concluded that I was responding to firm treatment. He was wrong. What was happening was that I was beginning to believe in my dream.

It was one of those slapstick Ciccio and Ingrassia films which gave me my next idea, which was this: I would creep up behind Carlo and hit him judiciously on the head. The blow must not be fatal but must be hard enough to knock him out cold. While he was out cold I would tie him up. Next I would drag him down to the cellar where I would keep him a prisoner on bread and water making him do my will.

Puerile, Signora? But remember where Carlo is now.

I didn't for a moment think I would do it. My fantasies were —I thought—purely therapeutic. They kept me from breaking up a marriage which I wanted to keep going. They helped me through what I thought of as a bad patch. Because something was sure to turn up soon. Carlo would get a transfer to some proper city where I would find work and where we would have friends and more money. It was just a matter of hanging on.

As the dream grew too familiar, I had to keep escalating it. Like a drug, I had to up the dose, and like ink in water it began slowly to spread until it was thinly colouring my waking life. The first actual move I made was to buy some pieces of old lead piping from the *ferraiuolo*. They were quite short, about a foot long. I told him I was going to do an assembly of metal scraps as a sort of garden sculpture. That sort of thing was popular enough and he was not surprised. Instead, I wrapped each separate piece of piping in a number of old socks and hid it. Piece number one was in our bedroom below my underwear. Piece two was in the kitchen behind the pressure-cooker. A third was in a drawing-room vase. And so on. The idea was that next time Carlo and I began to fight I would put my cellar plan into effect.

It must start with a row. I must have provocation. This was riskier than just creeping up on Carlo when he was reading the paper or eating breakfast, but the game, I felt, had rules. *He* must hit me first.

Oddly—or perhaps understandably?—our rows slackened off after I bought the lead piping. When we were sitting in, say, the dining-room a tiff would begin to simmer and danger, unknown to Carlo, would loom. There was, for instance, the time he complained about the pasta and asked how long did it take an intelligent woman to learn to time it? His sister had known how to cook pasta since she was eight and he had no doubt I thought myself cleverer than she. Behind his back, in the cutlery drawer of the walnut sideboard, wrapped innocuously in a damask napkin, lay piece of lead piping number four. All I had to do—but I don't have to tell you. I gloated—and conciliated.

"Well," he heckled, "deny it. Deny that you think Giovanna is a dumb little thing."

"I do deny it."

"Can't you sound more convincing?" His fork was embedded in glutinous spaghetti. He tried to extricate and wind a few tubes. They broke. "Glue!" he spat. "Giovanna . . ."

"I *like* Giovanna."

"You'd like to influence her. I must say I admire your gall. You're only two years older than she. You don't understand this country." (Another poke at the congealing mess.) "Yet you take it upon yourself to lecture her."

"You weren't supposed to be listening."

"Well I was."

"Anyway *she* was lecturing *me*."

Giovanna of course is *your* spy, Signora! Your victim, doll, mouthpiece and punching-ball. Poor Giovanna. She's waiting to be married before settling down to being one person. Meanwhile there's no trusting her. She and I—though she may deny that now—got on quite well. Alone together, we both let ourselves say a little too much. I liked drawing her. She has that frail blonde Florentine beauty and it bothered me to think how some sexy brute like Carlo will one day squash her flat. *I* enjoyed Carlo's juicy gaminess, but I'm tough, whereas you brought poor Giovanna up to be subservient. Oh yes, you did. Can you deny that when we stayed with you, you always got her to iron Carlo's shirts? Over my protests, of course.

"Oh," you said, laughing, "it's good practice for when she'll be married."

Putting *me* in my place.

16

"Una", you said, "is an artist. She designs shirts. We can't expect her to iron them."

The galled jade winced.

"You're an artist," said Giovanna the day Carlo—as it turned out—was eavesdropping. "So it's different for you. Besides, you're not a Catholic. Nobody has to be a Catholic. It's a free choice. If you make it, you live by it."

We were talking about birth-control.

"Tell me," I asked, "when were *you* offered a choice? To be a Catholic or, for that matter, a woman?"

"Or", threw back Giovanna, "to be alive at all. But I *am* alive and if I live I ought to do it coherently. If I try to change the rules, I'll make a fool of myself. I have no power. The best *I* can do is conform elegantly. That's the civilized way."

"You have power over your own body."

"Uncontrolled appetites", Giovanna stated, "are obscene. One must practise restraint. What would you think of a glutton who pierced a hole in his belly, evacuating the masticated food through a pipe—let me finish! Through a pipe into, say, a disposable plastic bag so that he could go on ingurgitating more unnecessary edibles? The idea disgusts you, doesn't it? Well *I* feel the same disgust at the idea of a man evacuating all that risk-free sperm into a disposable plastic container!" (Had she got the hideous image, do you suppose, Signora, from some preacher at that convent school you sent her to? Or was it some lewd local confessor who fanned her scruples with his prurient, garlicky breath?)

"But, Giovanna," I answered, "if your husband doesn't do it with you he'll do it elsewhere. *You've* been brought up to control yourself but the male half of the population has not. Assuming that you *can* control yourself once you get married —which is highly questionable—no Italian male is going to accept the same restraints for himself."

We argued it back and forth and it ended up with Giovanna having a crying fit.

"I'm asking you", said Carlo next day, "to leave Giovanna alone. She must wonder about *me* after the way you talked. She must think I'm a sex maniac."

"Come off it, Carlo, the only thing wrong with Giovanna is that she's a virgin, twenty-two years old, idle and living with her mother. She's bursting with repressed sex. Put a match to her and she'd explode. All she needs is a few months on her own in Paris or London."

"If ever I leave you", said Carlo, "you should try your hand as a pimp. It's a good refuge for sex-obsessed women in their decline."

When he is as nasty as that I know I have him. He has lost his cool and I can toast him on the spit of his contradictions. For Carlo—did you know?—is an uncomfortable hybrid. He's two-thirds cool cat, a third residual Latin. The cool cat carries the Latin like a caudal growth: something disagreeable and reversionary whose removal would require painful surgery. It makes him easy to torment. But I forbore. Piece of piping number four restrained me. I savoured the responsibilities of power.

I was going to tell you about the shackles.

That purchase was a consequence of my earlier one. The *ferraiuolo* decided I was obviously a good market and took to showing me his most unpromising junk. I suspect he sold my name—there is a trade in such tips—to other pedlars as a likely gull, for all sorts of beggars, tripe-vendors, rag-and-bone men, gipsies and tramps began to call. None of them had anything I wanted until one day, about three months after I bought the lead piping, the *ferraiuolo* himself turned up with an object which he assured me would figure marvellously in an artistic assemblage. It was a set of fetters. Or perhaps two sets. I'm not sure since I could never decide whether they were intended for shackling one four-footed or two two-footed animals or perhaps merely the rear hooves of two four-footed ones. Anyway there were two separate units involved. Each consisted of a pair of U-shaped pieces of iron with holes through which an iron bar was threaded. The iron bar itself was about five feet long and pierced at its extremities with holes through which stout chains were passed. These chains could be fastened by a padlock. Since each U-shaped fetter contained six holes in all, the bar could be threaded through at varying levels so as to diminish or enlarge its size. At their largest, the fetters would fit a man's ankles, at their smallest, a child's wrists.

"What were they for?" I asked the *ferraiuolo*.

He shrugged. "Maybe they were used in a slaughter-house? Or a stud? Maybe they were an instrument of torture? They're very well made anyway. Lovely handiwork! You won't get a finish like that nowadays. An odd object anyway. It'll intrigue people. Nobody will have seen another. They could even be part of some old historical object." The *ferraiuolo* waved his hand imaginatively. "Like, ah, I don't know, maybe a set of stocks, why not? *Un ceppo, sì.* Maybe I should try and sell them to an antique dealer, if you don't want them. I'm giving you first refusal because you're a customer, that's fair, isn't it? A night club might use them. They're suggestive."

"Mmm."

"Listen," the *ferraiuolo* tried humour. "If your husband has an eye for the women, you could use it to tie him by the leg, haha! I'm only joking; you understand, Signora. It's just my way. No offence meant."

"O.K.," I said. "I'll take them."

In fairness to myself, I think I should describe one of our rows—started, as it happens, by you. It was last December and you had driven over with your gilty Christmas gifts and gossip. An American friend of mine, you reported, had walked out on her Sicilian husband. *He* had retaliated by kidnapping their six-month baby and fleeing to Messina. An English girl who works at the British Institute had taken her in and, together with some left-wing lawyer friends, they were about to take legal action to recover the baby.

"Of course she hasn't a hope," you said. "A mother who leaves her husband has no rights at all."

"But surely *you*", I asked, "are on her side." In view of your regard for motherhood, I thought you might at least be on the fence.

"Me? No. Why? If she made a bad wife, she'd make a bad mother."

"How do you know she was a bad wife? Because she is an American?"

You dodged that one. Though you mayn't care for foreigners, you probably rate Sicilians a bit below them.

"A woman", you said, "who can't make a success of her marriage will never make one of child-rearing. A woman's first obligation is to her family. No matter what her husband does, *she* must work to keep it together. Your American friend made rather a mess of that, didn't she?" You shrugged.

The argument dwindled off. I forget the rest but have a strong image of you with your freshly highlit hair, bolt upright on our couch: a stiff old mummy decked in the pride of matriarchy and certitude. When you left, Carlo said I had been disagreeable. I denied this.

"She knows Mary-Lou is a friend of mine. She needn't have sounded so pleased."

"It's a matter of principle with her."

"Well I", I told him, "have principles, too. I think I was forbearing."

I went into the kitchen. I'm not domestic. I've gone through that phase. However, this year, I had made an effort and cooked a number of plum-puddings. Plum-pudding is one of the few English dishes foreigners like and I was going to serve one at Christmas, one at New Year and a third at Twelfth Night. The rest were for giving away. For the honour of old England I had gone to a lot of trouble, taking no short-cuts and making everything as traditional and genuine as possible. There were eight altogether ranged on the shelf in their cloth-covered bowls and I was looking at them now, realizing that I'd forgotten to give you yours to take with you. Suddenly, Carlo came charging into the kitchen. He had obviously been smouldering blackly for some minutes. The Mary-Lou case is the sort that can upset him badly. In a calm moment he would be totally on Mary-Lou's side and indignant at the anomalies of Italian justice. But let a foreigner—me—express that indignation first and Carlo can do an about-face in no time at all. Seeing me absorbed in admiration of my plum-puddings, he put up his fist and swept all eight of them from the shelf. Two broke. The cloth cover came off another so that it spilled its contents. Five were intact. He began kicking at these.

"Stop! Carlo!" I caught his shirt, pulling him away from my last puddings. He pulled backwards and the shirt tore. I clawed at it some more. It was silk, especially made for him in London and he was proud of it.

He began banging my head against the wall. I reached for his balls but he caught my elbows. . . .

No need to give you a blow-by-blow account. As usual, I was left, when he finally stormed out of the door, with bruises, a headache, a torn dress, no plum-puddings and a strong sense of injustice. He came back in a couple of hours and apologized, wept, accused himself—*and you*—said . . . What does it matter what he said? My nose was swollen and stayed that way for a week. My eyes had begun to have a permanent puff. Sooner or later he might disfigure me and what I resented and could not forgive was the permanent disparity between us, the superior muscle which he could use even when he was wrong and knew it. But—I didn't want to leave. There was my recurrent dilemma and we both had bad tempers.

I suspect—I *know*—that your favourite image of Carlo is as Mamma's little-boy in his First Communion photograph: about three feet high, squared shoulders, milk-toothy smile, "English-tailored" suit and great white rosette. No matter what I tell you, about the Carlo of today, you will close your eyes, shrink him back to manageable proportions and present him with that satin rosette for innocence. If innocence means ignorance of other people's needs, then Carlo certainly gets that rosette. If it means—as my dictionary would have it—"guileless or not injurious", he doesn't. Carlo's guilelessness is a self-deceiving act: guile camouflaging itself.

Shall I tell you more about our rows? They always started for no reason but the root-reason: resentment-left-from-the-row-before and ended with Carlo sitting on my chest weeping over the damage done to me and proclaiming his innocence.

"Una, *you know* I can't control myself when I get started. Why do you provoke me?"

"What's provocation?"

"Look at the state your face is in! Your looks are being ruined. Una, don't try to tangle with me! I beg you. Look, I *try* to hold myself in. I *do* hold myself back. You *know* that! Christ, if I were to let myself go I'd have killed you ten times over. *I'm stronger than you*, you silly bitch. *Madonna Santa!* You'll have to hide in the house for a week now or people will think I'm an animal! *Che figura!* Una, look at your neck! And your eye! Do you realize I could blind you? Why do you do this to us? Una? Why?"

Carlo wept a bit, caressed me a bit, blew his nose and began to talk again.

"Your trouble", said Carlo, "is that you're not sure of yourself as a woman. You're afraid to *let* yourself be womanly. But womanliness is a wonderful thing! Una, Una," his fingers promenaded my neck, "why do you look so ironic? Irony is the weapon of the timid, do you know that? Of the people who are afraid of the great—the simple things in life!" He had an erection. "Close your eyes," he whispered.

I did for a minute; then I opened them. Carlo had closed his. He was lying on his back, his head a piece of forgotten jetsam, his hips working, his teeth bared, laughing only in the sense that we sometimes say an animal "laughs". A line of verse swam into my head: "Those great sea-horses bare their teeth and laugh at the foam."

"Ha!" Carlo crowed. "You're liking it! Aren't you? Aren't you? You can't help yourself, can you? *Donna, sei troppo donna!* Ha-aaagh!"

After making love—not right after but in, say, three-quarters of an hour—Carlo tended to become testy, even truculent. He may have felt he needn't be pleasant any longer since he wouldn't need me again that day or he may have held some sort of grudge against me: a sense perhaps of loss. He usually began by taking back his earlier apologies.

"The truth of it is you're a masochist. You *like* me to hit you. What's more you know it gives you an advantage by making me feel bad. My mother always said . . ."

"Your mother . . ."

"Don't say a word against la Mamma! She sees through you

all right. It takes one woman to see through another!"

"If only she would keep out of our affairs! If only she would shut . . ."

"If *you* shut up we wouldn't have any problems. Women aren't *meant* to argue with men. Look, Una, in the natural world every animal has its weapon. Some are passive. Take the skunk or the hedgehog or the snail . . ."

"Pleasant company. Come on, you stupid bastard. Get up off my chest and get me a drink."

We'd probably laugh then and make up, but peace was precarious. Carlo was alert to the distinction between humouring and submission. He hated to be laughed at. He would try to laugh back but usually the laugh persisted until it became a bellow.

"Sense of humour," he would begin in an amused voice. "The great British invention: weapon of the inarticulate. When in doubt, laugh. It covers a multitude, doesn't it? Especially it covers snobbery, because one always laughs *down, vero*? One laughs at the inferior, the mildly grotesque! No *proof* of one's own superiority is needed. The laugh does it all: Haha, haha, ha!" He rushed at me suddenly. "Haha!" he howled.

"You're hurting me again!"

"Laugh while I'm hurting you. Let's see the sense of humour working while I hurt you! Mmm? Not so easy? Why don't you laugh!"

"I'm waiting for you to cry."

"Me? Cry?"

"Didn't you know you always do? It's your gimmick. I laugh. You cry. Tears," I would howl, for by now he would be twisting my arm or pulling out handfuls of my hair, "tears prove, ha, sensibility. Stoppit, you bastard! You're a repentance addict," I yelled, "you got hooked at the time of your First Communion when they gave you that nice white rosette. Stop, you're breaking my arm."

And so on. Only the venue changed. Once we fought in the bathroom of a party in Florence where Carlo thought I had been flirting with a bearded hippy and I got so messed up that Carlo had to bribe the hired help to smuggle us out at the back.

Another time when we were fighting in one of the backstreets of Volterra—cowboy-style we had left a trattoria to finish things outside—a policeman challenged us. Carlo explained that he was my husband and merely arranging his domestic troubles in the only way that seemed to work. The policeman was welcome to see our identity cards if he wished. The policeman did. He may have thought I was a whore or Carlo a molester of women. However, when he saw the cards, he agreed with some embarrassment—Southern gallantry may have been a touch uncomfortable—that, yes, a husband did, in effect, have certain rights, though not exaggerated ones nowadays—"*Siamo un popolo civile*"—such matters *were* better settled within the family domicile, but the law was chary of . . . well, yes . . . Good evening Signor Dottore, Signora . . . He retreated.

Carlo lies dead.

I hit him too hard. I finally hit him and, in spite of being wrapped in three of his own old socks, the piece of lead piping smashed his skull. Maybe his skull was one of those freak ones: paper-thin. Some English literary figure, I forget which, fell backwards off his chair and cracked his skull and died. The autopsy revealed that the bone had been so thin that the slightest tap could have killed him at any point in his life. Maybe Carlo's too was paper-thin? But will the Italian police find this out? Will they consider it an attenuating circumstance?

"*Commissario*"—should I say *brigadiere*? What *are* they called? What? *Maresciallo* perhaps?—"I swear I never meant to kill him."

The *Commissario* has heard that one before.

Carlo lies limp, blood oozing thickishly through the roots of his hair. The neighbours crowd in: all women at this hour. They wear housecoats or else carry string-bags full of green-groceries and udder-shaped flasks for oil. They stare at the unnatural foreign woman who has killed such a fine man, such a decent, good-looking stud lost now forever to their timid lusts.

"Gesummaria!"
"Che strage!"

I could say it was passion. Passion-crimes are respected in Italy, leniently punished. Jealousy? Say he was sleeping with one of the neighbours. Which? They all look ready for it: tumid, womanly women. It might even be true. They'd deny it, though, band together, make a liar of me. And then: are Englishwomen *allowed* passion? Madness more likely: *pazza inglese*, mad Englishwoman. The photographers are being let in. Flash. Shall I look mad? Throw myself on the corpse? Cry, scream? No. Close my eyes. It *was* passion. It *was*. Not their sort, perhaps, but passion, yes. I could have left if I had not been so possessive: just said, "Good-bye, Carlo, sorry it didn't work out better. I shall remember you fondly." He'd have found someone else. The shit! *Stronzo!* This way he's mine—for all he's worth. Cut off his head, shall I, and plant it in a pot of basil? A bit disgusting really. There's no death penalty in Italy but they have *mediaeval* prison conditions. I've read about them: scandalous. How shall I get out of this? The policeman is writing his *verbale*. Words from the crime columns of the evening papers agglomerate like flies on jam: black flies attracted by the jammy blood of Carlo. *L'imputata*, that's me: the accused. But I have accused myself. I rang the police. Will that count in my favour? I should have a lawyer. Don't say another word until I get one. The moment I put down the phone I started bashing myself up, trying to leave convincing bruises. I threw myself against furniture, beat myself black and blue with a belt—beautiful variegated welts. I wanted to have a black eye but I hadn't the nerve. (Try punching *yourself* in the eye!)

"We were having a fight, *Signor Commissario*. I reached for something, I didn't know what to hit him with. I was mad, blinded with pain, not thinking, *Signor Commissario!* He was much stronger than I!" Look at my bruises, my torn hair, my dress in ribbons—pity about that eye! "It turned out to be the meat mallet!" (As you might imagine I'd got rid of the bits of lead piping. Down the well.) "Poor Carlo, I never thought . . . I bought that mallet only a month ago. It's made of boxwood.

I got it to flatten veal so as to make thin, thin veal scallops for him, cooked with sage the way he liked them. In oil. . . ." Distraught wife! "How could I imagine. I didn't even aim, *Signor Commissario!* He was twisting my other arm. Look at the bruises! And then . . . it happened before I knew it. How *could* I . . . Poor, poor Carlo went down like a sack of potatoes!" Not a good simile. Stop. Cry a bit.

Clever Una did remember to smarm a little of Carlo's bloody hair on the mallet. Oh, we have all read the crime columns. *La cronaca nera.* But do they tell all? I'm manic. Maybe they *will* find me mad? I regret Carlo's death but less—considerably less—than the loss of Carlo alive. The crime of passion is the meanest of all: ungenerous, grasping, crime of the weak and the unloved. It should be doubly punished, not less. My blood fizzles in my veins. Murder exhilarates. Power thrills. Meanwhile I am afraid. And sorry. All at once. I have an urge to talk. Mustn't talk, might incriminate myself. Beware. Everything I say may be written down and used as evidence. Twenty years I might get for this. *L'ergastolo.* And the one I really want to tell about it all is Carlo, Carlo, Carlo. . . .

"Una, wake up! You're shouting!"

Carlo is shaking me, laughing at me.

"What's the matter with you, Una? You're completely bonkers! Shouting in your sleep! Do you know what you shouted: '*Pazza inglese!*' Honestly!" He laughs witlessly. The light bulb hangs nakedly over our double bed. For a year I have been promising to make a Victorian-type ruffled lace shade for it and never did. Naturally. Because I never *do* anything, do I? I only dream of doing. Carlo is still shaking me even though I am awake. He thinks it very funny that I should talk in my sleep. He has a smug, placid look.

"You were talking about yourself, weren't you? Calling yourself the mad Englishwoman? *Pazza inglese!*" He laughs. "Poor Una, *poverina, va!*" He has a superior look. His superiority sticks in my craw.

I pull away from him, leap up, clutch the flex by which the bulb hangs, yank it out of the ceiling and smash the hot bulb down on Carlo's head. There is a satisfying smashing sound and

we are in the dark. Have I killed him? What if his skull . . . ?
But no, he has leaped on me, all sweaty thirteen stone of him,
he's squeezing my throat and rolling me on a sheet covered
with smashed glass. My eyes dazzle from the after-glare of the
bulb. I try to scream but he's strangling me.

"You mad bloody bitch! Mad is right. I could kill you.
DO YOU REALIZE THAT?"

He lets go. I am choking. My body is scratched all over by
the glass and there is no light. I crawl into the bathroom and
vomit, then sit, shivering on the lavatory. Mindless.

I look at the mirror. There are bruises on my throat. Fresh
bruises. They will get more dramatic. My back and thighs are
streaked with blood from the glass. Now would be the time
to show myself. *Signor Commissario.* . . . Ah no! No more
fantasy. There *does* lie the way to madness. The weak fantasize
and resign themselves.

Coldly, deliberately and with no sense of release, I take out
the piece of lead piping that I keep in the lavatory cistern, dry
it in a towel and use it to smash the bathroom mirror in which
I have just been contemplating myself. It is six feet square and
less than a year old. Smash! The blow is not on a level with
murder but is at least a real act. I leave the piping in the wash-
basin and go to sleep in the spare room.

You see, Signora, I was obsessed. I had him, as the French
say, in my skin. Like a burr. His image was stuck in the folds
of my brain.

You can't live on sex and the memory and expectation of it
but, once we came to Volterra, there was little else for me to
do. Mine was worse than a harem-life. Harems have other
women in them.

Men used to follow me in the streets. I had that free, foreign
look. They had that furtive Italian disease of desire. Their
pockets bulged as they fingered their genitalia—Americans
call this "playing pocket-pool"—and their trousers were always
too tight. Thin gabardine suits covered but outlined their flesh.

"Do you like Italy?" they hissed. "Do you like Italian men?"

"No."

I did not like Italian or any other category of men. I was riveted by a resentful passion to one man. I resented his violence, also his having filled my mind with trivia, interrupted my independent life and drawn me into the game of playing house. I had enjoyed this while it was novel, never seeing the drudgery in it. During my first months with Carlo—in Rome before we got married—I willingly spent hours making salads which were edible mosaics and got up at seven to go marketing. Every act was pleasurable. It was as if some bolt had been adjusted in my body heightening all my senses. I could not tell whether the agency was sex with Carlo or swimming at Fregene or listening to a baroque concert in some old court-yard. Or even the food? I was seduced by basil smells and the gibbous gleam on an egg-plant. That summer went by in a welter of animal gratification. I don't think I read a book. I certainly never bought a newspaper. My mind slept and while it did I contracted for a life which left it little scope.

As an Italian, you can never experience that first stultifying impact of Italy and its pleasures. You know them too well: their techniques, how to dose them and how to make them tick. You are amused by the speed with which we succumb. *L'arte della vita*, that self-congratulatory phrase, celebrates your adroitness at dealing with the body. "*Vi piace L'Italia?*" you ask. "Do you like our country?" The question is pure rhetoric. You know we do, and our liking is often so gluttonous that you manage to feel spiritually superior as well. Our later dis-satisfactions escape you or you put them down to a dyspeptic inability to live. To Puritanism. O.K. The word is as good as another. Its residue in me is a need for balance: a need to think as well as feel, to structure my life. I will *not* spend it plotting the best ways to serve the senses and making endless trips to little knitting women and trimming women and little men in the hills who can sell me demijohns of unadulterated olive oil or wine or rounds of *pecorino*. I know all this is necessary if food and clothes are to be exquisite. But the price is too high. I choose against *l'arte della vita*. From now on I shall buy my dresses ready-made and nobody in England will notice that the two-millimetre dip of my left shoulder has not been countered by an especially constructed pad. I shall forget the distinction between good and less good oil. I renounce a repetition of that summer with Carlo: sensual ecstasy, the incandescent pinnacle of what Italy has to give. I tear myself away from him while I still want him—and I don't see Carlo as a hook on which to hang sensations. I love *him*. Himself. His every tic and inch of flesh is photographed on my retina. Possessively. Tenderly. With lust. But he can't be separated from the life here—he wouldn't come with me and, if he did, it wouldn't work. My feeling for him has turned poisonous. I have to go and let him go.

At the time I was telling you about I hadn't come round to accepting this.

I had the shackles. I put them on my own legs: sourly modelling them. They cut my shins. If ever they were to be used they must be padded. I cut up a red velvet cushion—cardinal-red, rather pretty; I had made it during my playing-house phase. Now I used it to swathe and upholster the shackles. I thought of other things while I sewed. Then I hid them.

The *ferraiuolo* meanwhile sold me an iron bedstead with a wrought-iron back and base: one of those period extravaganzas in which twining vines and fronds fan out from an enamelled picture—this one is of the Madonna—in a network more appropriate for a gate or balustrade than for a bed back. They are usually brass. This one is iron. As you know they are fashionable again and fairly expensive. However, I happened to have received a cheque from my mother a little time before. Her second family absorbs most of her attention but when she does think of me she is quite generous.

I got the *ferraiuolo* to help me down to the cellar with it, telling him that I was keeping it as a surprise for my husband's birthday. He assembled it and I put a mattress on it and laid the shackles on the mattress. Then—as though I had paid my fantasy sufficient tribute—I managed to put it out of my mind.

Next came a goodish period. Carlo and I went to Milan for a fortnight and were quite close. When we came back I found I'd skipped a period. I didn't tell him. Here, Signora, is the page I promised you in my note:

Carlo, as you know, insisted on our having a church wedding. I agreed easily. I was in love with him and with Italy and a church wedding seemed the appropriate ceremony to celebrate both loves. Its binding nature did not bother me since, as a non-Catholic, I could disregard its purely spiritual bonds the day the marriage proved unworkable. I could get an English divorce. I fully expected that this might happen. My mother and father are divorced and quite happily remarried, so divorce has always seemed normal to me. First marriages—my mother calls them "trial marriages"—especially between foreigners are often impermanent. The words of the marriage ceremony are to me pure ritual: nicely put but rescindable. It follows that I had no intention of getting pregnant by Carlo. Unknown to him, I had been on the pill from the time we started living together. Unfortunately, I did not always take it regularly—no subconscious conflict here, just plain sloppiness. So when my period didn't come I was worried. Having no friends in Volterra, I had no way of finding an abortionist there and no money to pay one if I did. It looked as though I might have to go to England for an abortion and, as getting the money and setting up a cover-story for my trip were likely to take time, I had plenty of reasons for anxiety. You may imagine my mood. By the way—I have letters to and from my mother written when I was contemplating marriage to Carlo. They prove that my attitude at the time really was the one I have just described.

Okay? Do remember to extract this page and send it to your canon-lawyer friend. I remind you lest the rest of this missive end in the incinerator or be torn to ribbons by your enraged and thriftless fingers. But do read on before doing anything unconsidered. This document is not being written purely for my sake but also for a purpose which must jibe with your own: it is a barrier to keep me from coming back.

You know—or perhaps you don't, so let me tell you—that between a man and a woman who are deeply involved sexually —I shy a little doubtfully at this stage from that puff-ball word "love"—atrocious injuries can be forgiven. It is not impossible that Carlo and I, *even now*, might be reconciled. You don't believe this? You think me simple-minded? But you have not experienced the perverse pleasures of our fighting-life. I forgave him repeatedly. He forgave me—oh yes, Signora, even before my lead-pipe days, I managed to give back something of what I got—acutely embarrassing scenes in which he cut a wretched figure before friends. *Brutta figura!* Into that Achilles heel, the rotting soft spot of the vain I could always stick a claw!

It is to that same vulnerability, his fear of *brutta figura*, that this letter is addressed. By letting you, la Mammina, into our noisome secrets, it makes it harder for Carlo to forgive me. Forgive-and-forget is a package deal. But who can forget when there is a witness close to one who knows all and reminds one that she does by constant jibes? I rely on you for this. You will keep him from me and me from him—which, sadly, is what we need.

It occurred to me that if I did have to make a trip to England, Carlo would be alone in the house; he might visit the cellar and see the objects there. I was acutely embarrassed at the thought. Fantasies and their props are private: painfully so. At least they are for me. While fantasy stays in one's head, it is safe. Once it has confronted reality—like now—shame no longer attaches to it. At the intermediary stage at which mine had got stuck, while my props lay unused in the cellar, discovery can only be humiliating.

I decided to do away with the fetters. The bed was not compromising. I would pretend I had bought it as a surprise and was keeping it for Carlo's birthday or our anniversary. Indeed, as I thought about it, I became convinced that this was the truth. But the fetters with their home-sewn red velvet padding would be harder to explain. They must be got rid of. The question was how? The Volterra town council had recently been issuing plastic bags for householders' rubbish and our rubbishmen were no longer prepared to deal with the heavy old dustbins. My fetters with their bars and chains would not fit into the new little bags. I could throw them into our well but it was sometimes cleaned and they might be dragged up again in the spring. I could not bear the thought. Burying them was just as risky. The thing to do was to put them into the boot of the car, drive into the country and drop them somewhere. Unfortunately, just as I came to this conclusion, our old Giulietta got battery trouble and had to be hauled off to the garage for a week.

It was during this week that my scenario escaped me. I had decided to scrap it and instead it began to act itself out.

Carlo got a notion that we ought to put down some wine. A friend of his had joined some club which imported French wines at cut prices. This, the friend claimed, was a once-in-a-decade year for Rhine—or Rhône? I wouldn't remember—wines. He advised Carlo to buy all he could afford and put it down. Carlo decided to inspect our cellar.

"The bulb's broken," I told him. "I've been meaning to get the yard man to change it. It's too high for me. I'll get him to do it in the morning."

"I'll do it. I know where he keeps the ladder."

"Carlo, you'll fall. Let him do it."

This was the wrong tack. Vanity, the old weak spot, must not be injudiciously touched. Carlo gave a manly laugh, equipped himself with torch and ladder, and set off down the cellar stairs. I ran down behind him. It was wonderful, I said sarcastically into the blackness, how pathetically true to type he ran. Putting down wine indeed when we hadn't enough money to run a decent car. Was he laying it up for his children's baptism parties, assuming we ever had any?

Carlo set up his ladder. In one hand he held a fresh bulb, in the other his torch. He shone it around. Its beam caught the curlicues of the bed.

"What's that?" he asked indifferently, and began to climb the ladder. "I'll have this bulb in in a jiffy. Switch on the light when I tell you."

"You're not even listening!" I screamed. There was no-where for me to hide those fetters which would be in full, disgraceful view the moment I switched on the light. "You might discuss this with *me* before earmarking all our money for useless, snobby French wine! Damn you, Carlo, will you answer!"

Carlo removed the old bulb. He was having trouble holding

the torch and keeping his balance on the ladder. "I need three hands," he said. "What are you on about now?"

"Come down, Carlo, *please*! I want to talk to you. Now!" I shook the ladder.

He fell. His head banged against the iron bedpost and he lay very still. He had knocked himself out.

It was funny: sickly so, if you like. You see I might never have done it! I think I wouldn't have. I was so terrified of breaking his conceivably paper-thin cranium and then—my guardian angel or bad spirit did it for me. Ah well. Of course you are thinking and saying and will endlessly repeat—I can hear you as I write!—that what I should have done at this point was to ring a doctor. I had ample time now to find a temporary hiding-place for the shaming fetters and even if I had not, Carlo's health, his very life, you will say, demanded a doctor.

Well, as it turned out: they didn't. Carlo was right as rain in an hour. When he came to, lying on the bed, his feet threaded through the fetters—I had used them after all—the worst he was suffering from was a headache. In no time at all, I will admit, he was suffering from incredulity, shock, rage and sheer, unmanning bewilderment. He had no stomach for cunning that day. He failed to play the one card which would have won his release: it never occurred to him to pretend he was badly hurt.

No need to tell you about our first conversations. Carlo will describe them. I imagine I have left you matter for several years' chat—unless the subject is declared taboo. Even if it is, it will stick around: a memory responsive to hints and nudges.

Quickly then: there were rages, roars, sulks and refusals to speak. Unfairly, he looked his worst: cheeks fat with fury and black with a stubble of beard. Only on the third day did he think of reasoning with me:

"How do you think you're going to get away with this?"

"I don't expect to."

"Then why are you doing it? What do you expect to gain?"

C   33

"Only what I've got now."

"*What* have you got? You must want to force me to do something! *What?*"

"Nothing. I just want you like this."

"To humiliate me?"

"You could call it that."

"And what the hell do you think is going to happen when you release me?"

I had no answer to that one.

He was quite confident at first. He couldn't believe I'd keep it up or that someone wouldn't hear him or wonder where he was and come looking for him. He shouted a lot the first day or two, but I played the radio full-blast upstairs to show him how badly sound carried. With the basement and cellar doors shut, he couldn't hear *it*, so there was little chance of anyone's hearing *him*. Gradually he gave that up. Still, he relied on his colleagues wondering about his sudden disappearance from the office. I told him I had written a letter of resignation purporting to come from him, explaining that an opportunity to work in London was being offered him by his stepfather-in-law, that he had had to take a sudden decision, was sorry for the inconvenience caused but hoped they would understand.

"I forged your signature. I'd been practising."

"The letter's sure to be full of appalling grammar. They'll know there's something wrong."

"No, it's all formulas. I looked through your files of old correspondence and lifted all the ready-made office jargon I could. I write better Italian than I speak. You can see the rough copy if you like."

"They'll think it extraordinary my giving notice like that."

"They'll be annoyed but they won't investigate. People never do."

They didn't. Apart from one phone call which I answered saying yes, Carlo was in London, no, he didn't plan on getting back soon, we heard nothing from the office. Later in the week I went in to collect a few of his things and repeated my story to two of his colleagues. If they thought about Carlo at all, they probably thought he had been too embarrassed to show his face, envied him his influential father-in-law and forgot about him.

What followed was totally different from the scene imagined in my dream-scenario. *There* action had been fast and satisfying. I triumphed. Carlo cringed. I, like God, was in control. I spoke persuasively and Carlo saw my point. I was free. The choices were mine. Instead: I was *not* free since I was afraid to release Carlo. I disliked myself, had strong feelings of nausea, was not persuasive and, in fact, hardly spoke. My mind, as though it had been I and not Carlo who had fallen on my head, was in a state of stunned lethargy. It could cope with no more than the mechanics of the situation, the physical routine required to keep the *status quo*: answering phone calls and letters, buying food, emptying his slop bucket, et cetera. When it came to thinking of the future, thought switched off. When he reasoned with me or tried to cajole me, I shrugged. I had imagined that I would use the time I held him prisoner to explain my grudges, to make him *see* how intolerable it can be to be always on the losing side, the weak partner, the one who must submit. I think I had supposed that his own position would make this clear to him in an immediate way. Zing! Message lodges in brain. Dominant partner apprehends reality of subject partner. True dialogue based on a shared premiss can now commence.

Haha! Permit me to laugh, Signora. It is at myself. Nothing of the sort happened or—I began to see—was likely to unless Carlo was kept chained to the bed for ten years. Chained up or free, Carlo was still Carlo—in the short run anyway—and I was still myself.

I began to understand this on the fourth day.

We had begun to settle into a routine. Carlo was letting me feed him—at first he had refused to eat. I was looking after him, necessarily, in a more intimate way than I ever had before and this aroused inappropriately motherly feelings in me. I found myself cooking his favourite food, worrying about his comfort and generally behaving more like the tender-hearted daughter of the despot in prototypal prison stories than like the implacable despot himself. *He* noticed this eventually—one thing that might be said to have been achieved was that Carlo had to start studying me and wondering how I ticked. He was learning the techniques of the underdog.

On the sixth day I came down with his lunch and found him reading a paperback I had left for him. I had not used the second pair of shackles for his arms but had looped their chain around his elbows attaching these behind his back to the bed back, then bringing the chain forward to circle his neck so that if he tried to pull his arm free the pressure would be on his own throat. His hands however were free and he could eat, drink, hold a book and manœuvre himself towards the slop bucket. The iron bar threaded through his leg-fetters was itself pierced by chains which hung down, one on the left the other on the right side of the bed, and were padlocked together underneath. These chains were long enough to allow him to adjust his position by moving to the right or left or by bending his knees as he had done on this occasion so as to form a support for his book.

"Do you want lunch?"

"You know what I want."

"Do you want lunch?"

"How the hell can I eat lunch? My neck is rubbed raw by this bloody chain. Every move I make it rubs. I could strangle myself in my sleep. What are you trying to do? Unman me? Why don't you castrate me and be finished? *You*'ll probably be locked up in a lunatic asylum for life when they get you. Do you want *me* to have to join you there? A fine future for us. Tell me, I can't think why I never asked: is there madness in your family?"

"I'm the mad Englishwoman, you've driven me mad!"

"Christ, you are at that!"

"Do you want lunch?"

"Una, it's *you* I worry about. I keep puzzling: *what did I do?* I mean tiffs and squabbles don't normally lead to this sort of thing as far as is generally known. Or do they in England? Is there a whole, submerged, unreported section of people's lives where the primitive urges are given leeway? Incest? Mayhem? Murder perhaps?"

The ironic look on Carlo's face slipped. He had frightened

himself. Murder *was*, after all, one logical way for me to get myself out of the fix I had got into.

"Una," it was a little boy's voice. "Una . . . I . . ."

I watched him watch me as I stood there with the cooling *lasagne*. I could see doubt ooze through him.

"Give me the lunch." He ate it silently, wiped his lips with the napkin I had brought, shot me one shifty look, then another. "That was . . . good . . . Una?"

I took his plate and left, shutting cellar and basement doors carefully behind me. When I reached the kitchen I smashed the dirty plate hard into the sink, sat down at the table and rested my face against its scrubbed surface. So this was where we were at now! He thought I *was* mad! Was trying to humour me. Shared premiss indeed! We were communicating less than before. What a laugh! We never seemed to get our wires uncrossed.

"You don't know how to talk *to* people!" I accused him some hours later. "You talk *at* them or get round them. You don't respect anyone enough to try and meet them half-way —certainly not your mother. Not Giovanna. Let's not mention me. It's the same with your men friends. You either tease them or defer to them. You trust nobody."

He looked tired. "Go on. Make yourself a good conscience. Blacken me. Do whatever it is you have to do."

"Do? What should I have to do? You're so suspicious!"

"I'd be a moron if I weren't. Una . . . why don't you go and see a doctor? I can't get out, can I? Go and visit Dottor Pietri. You needn't tell him what you've done to me, just that you're feeling . . . depressed, nervous. Get him to give you a checkup."

"Carlo, it's not *me*! It's *you*! Why do you think I had to do this?"

"I DON'T KNOW!" he shouted. "TELL ME!"

"Because you never saw me. Because you treated me like an automat, a penny-in-the-slot machine. Kiss it or stick your penis in it and it goes 'mmmgh!', hit it and it goes 'ow', set it for the dinner-at-eight schedule and it will comply. In case of breakdown send it to Dottor Pietri."

"You *are* mad."

"Well that's convenient, isn't it? Much easier to assume the trouble's all in me than have to assess your own life."

"Are you enjoying this?"

"No."

"Then what's the point of the exercise?"

There wasn't any. I realized this now. But it was too late to stop it. My power over Carlo was purely negative. I couldn't make him think or feel differently. He's cast in your mould. Doubts are alien to him. But releasing him straightaway would be too great a risk. What happened some days later underlined that. They had been uneventful days. Carlo ate, listened to his transistor radio, sulked, tried wheedling me a bit, had a tantrum, sulked, wheedled me again. His moods went in cycles. He was getting more anxious, however, as it became clear that his office had accepted my letter and that there was no immediate prospect of anyone discovering what was going on. He had been in the cellar ten days when Giovanna rang up. You and she were off to Austria next day on your skiing holiday and she wanted to give me your address there and say good-bye. I must have been a bit constrained on the phone. Carlo, I of course told her, was out. I'd tell him she'd rung. No, no point ringing back. He'd been invited to go duck shooting with some friends and was spending the night with them. He might be away two days. They were not on the phone. Duck shooting? Yes, I said, he'd just taken it up. These friends had introduced him to it. People we'd met at a party. They had no phone. He would certainly write and tell her all about it. Giovanna said oh, well, O.K., give him our love. I said enjoy yourself. She bridled. The skiing holiday is part of your get-Giovanna-well-married campaign and she knows I know this and is touchy. Also she knows that Carlo and I could do with some of the money you spend like water—but this is by the way. I only mention it to show how she came to associate the constraint in our conversation with herself and *her* concerns rather than with me and mine. "I wish I weren't going," she said at the end, "but you know how la Mamma is!" She had accepted the duck-shooting story easily. I went down and told Carlo.

I suppose this made him despair. It meant I had three weeks ahead of me during which I need have no fear of discovery. It must have seemed like an eternity. He was complaining of cramps already. Now he began to complain again of the chain on his neck. His complaints distressed me. I have already mentioned that I had begun to feel motherly about him. After all: I cleaned, fed, babied him. Perhaps I felt as you do towards him? I don't know. My resentments were gone. (Who can call a baby to account?) My mind swung between terror at what he might—would—do to me if I let him loose and horror at what I was doing to him. Yes, yes, I had begun admitting to myself that eventually I would have to go and, from some safe distance, telephone someone to come and set him free. But go where? Telephone who? The world outside our house had become unreal to me. I felt bound to this nasty riveting nest of my own fabrication, could not bear to go leaving such a memory behind. My possessiveness grew with his dependence and with the odd morbid gratitude—it may just have been cunning—with which he thanked me for my efforts to make him less uncomfortable. Usually, I took care to keep out of range of his hands which were, as I told you, free. On this day too I tried to examine his neck from a safe distance, but he seemed to have gone limp from exhaustion and his lolling head concealed the area which was being rubbed by the chain. I leaned closer. Suddenly his hand sprang up and grabbed my throat. They squeezed. I tried to shout but couldn't get my breath. He squeezed again, crushing my windpipe, railing at me ("*Stronza*, turd, mad bitch! I have you now!") and his eyes were stark and crazy. He had pulled the chain tight on his own neck which was in fact rubbed raw, but he seemed now to be unaware of this. Slowly his hands relaxed and he began to cry.

"I could . . .", he sobbed, "I could . . . Una, what have you done to us both? We're mad! We're both mad! This is degrading. It's valueless. It's against every value. Una, we were normal people, we . . . listen, Una, *ti prego*, I'll make any promise you like. But let me out. Look, I realize, I really do, that I must be to blame for some of this. As much as you. I was insensitive, I . . . But, look, this is destroying us both.

Can't you see that? Can't you, Una? Una, say something."

"You're choking me."

"What use is there in this, Una?"

"None."

"Listen," his stranglehold had turned into a sort of caress, but he was still holding me tightly and his own arms were held tightly to the bed so that our movements were restricted. "I could kill you," he whispered. "Don't you know that?"

"What good would that do you?"

"What good is any of this to anyone?"

His nervous excitement had found the usual outlet, he had begun trying to make love. But he was afraid to let go my neck. "Unbutton me," he whispered. I did. We managed to make love. I only tell you this, Signora, to show how hopelessly tangled up our emotions were: his as well as mine. We lived in a fetid bubble of dependence and rancour.

"Do you hate me?" he whispered now.

"No."

"We must trust each other."

"Yes."

"Fuck," he said, then, and then: "you're liking it. Go on: say it. Say it! SAY IT."

Was that strategy, Signora? I don't know, do I, any more now than I did then. I was enjoying it as I always did with Carlo. I was venting the pent humours of ten days. Slowly, his fingers uncurled so that I could move freely above him. At the end he was not restraining me at all.

"Carlo!" I wanted to weep.

"Where are the keys?"

"Upstairs."

"Go on up", he whispered, "and get them. Go on, Una."

I went upstairs to the kitchen and opened the drawer where I kept the keys. My neck was hurting where he had squeezed it. I turned to look in the kitchen mirror and saw the blackberry-juice outline of his ten fingers on my throat. I closed the drawer, leaving the keys inside and did not go back to the cellar again that day. Next morning I reconsidered the risks of releasing

Carlo. They did not seem to me any less than before. I went down and told him I did not intend to release him.

He didn't talk to me for thirty-six hours after that. He also refused to eat. But I did not, of course, give in. I won't say I was firm. Every moment was a flea's leap of doubt—but the effect was the same as if I had been stubbornly wedded to decision: Carlo did not get released. After the thirty-six hours, he asked for a drink. I gave him wine in which I had dissolved several sleeping pills. When he had been asleep for some time I approached him with great caution, blasted the transistor radio in his ear, poked him from a distance with a piece of wood and—lest he might be fooling—dangled a realistic trick-shop plastic scorpion close to his face. He did not wake up. I got my keys, unlocked the padlock on the chains which held his arms and neck, unlooped them and pulled him down to a supine position. Then I got my second set of fetters, pulled his wrists through them, fastened them in place by pulling the bar through the lower pair of holes in each fetter, laid the entire contraption across his thighs so that his arms were parallel to his body, threaded the chains through the ends of the bar and padlocked them together under the bed as I had already done with the foot-fetters. This meant Carlo could now actually move more. He could sit up or lie down by displacing the bars whose attaching chains were fairly long, and could edge over to the side of the bed to use his slop bucket. His hands, however, were free only from the wrist. It would be harder for him to make a grab at me. While he was asleep, I brought down a basin of water and washed him all over. Then I powdered him with Roberts talcum powder. He was turning more and more into my baby: my battered baby. It humiliated me since it must him. I, who resent the body's weaknesses—remember; the source of all our trouble was my lack of muscle—had now inflicted intolerable bodily constraints on Carlo. Ironically, that very day, I found one of my own constraints had gone: my overdue period arrived. The pregnancy—*my* fetter—had either never been or had terminated itself. Who knew? One knows so little about the biological processes—and when I say "one" I don't just mean "I". Doctors are as vague as any female. "Maybe you had a little miscarriage and mistook it for a heavy period," they'll say when questioned. "Maybe you are just irregular?" Shrug, smile; what does it matter? Get on with it. It's the curse of Eve. *I* saw a meaning here, however. My release was a nod from Fate, old *ignis fatuus* who lurks in the madder mathematical corners of my mind making his own kind of sense. This was a *quid pro quo*. Fate helps those who help themselves. Fetter your husband, said the sign, and Fate will unfetter you. The equation comes out evenly if X is added in one place and subtracted in another. I had been approved! I have to break into my narrative here, Signora, to remind you that superstitions are only metaphors. I am no madder than you when I make my own signs and patterns—they are a filing system for otherwise unrelated perceptions—no madder, I say, than you when you accept holus-bolus the ready-made metaphor of your religion. No, don't be angry. I am really trying to get through to you, not to mock you. Let me say it another way: the arrival of my period, the abrupt flow of menstrual blood had come too perfectly on time to be chance. Maybe something in myself had set it off: perhaps some nervous convulsion had caused the miscarriage of a real pregnancy or released the dam of a false one? Either way it had happened because of what I was doing to Carlo. The message was clear: my interests and his were in opposition. I must cut the knot of our love/hate. I must go.

I put off going. This was the twelfth day and Carlo was still asleep. It was the thirteenth when he woke up and found the new fetters on his wrists. I think that then a sort of apathy seized him. He had tried everything, it must have seemed to him: anger, reason, threats, appeals, tears. He had refused to eat. He gave up scheming now. He had grown meek and constipated; he claimed to feel constant nausea.

"I'll give you a glycerine suppository."

"Okay."

He let me stick it up his anus with my finger, giving no signs of shame or vindictiveness. As if I'd been a nurse. But was he apathetic or testing me in some way? I did not discover.

"Will you eat?"

"Yes."

"I'll have to feed you."

"Okay."

His apathy was more wearing on my nerves than his sulks or tantrums. Inaction was telling on us both but perhaps more on me since the choice dangled constantly in the corner of my brain: I *could* put an end to this. Release him. Go. But then the whole thing would have been a failure. Sometimes it seemed to be more fear of anti-climax than fear of Carlo which kept me there. I told myself I must hold out. Something might even now click in his brain. By using force on me he had invited like treatment. Since *my* use of force had resolved nothing, might he not see—glimpse, allow—that it never could or did? But *if* he saw this, would *I* believe he was seeing it? I would not. Yet craved an absolving word.

"What are you using for money?" he asked finally.

It was the fifteenth day. I was keeping notes carefully. This letter is based on them. Putting in time, I shopped, cooked, cleaned more than I ever had, wrote and rewrote drafts for this letter, packed, tried to keep away from Carlo. I felt occasional urges to hurt him, frequent ones to harangue him. I was sexually hungry for him. At night he filled every dream. I *was* leaving, however. I had prepared a telegram summoning you from Austria. Alternatively I might wait and send you a letter after you got back. I wrote that, too. It must be sent, if the telegram had not been, a few days after your return from Austria, a month after I first tied Carlo up: my last possible date for departure.

"What are you using for money?"

"I got some from my mother. I wrote and told her it was an emergency. It came last week."

"*You* can't earn any, can you?"

"No."

"So chaining me up didn't change much, did it? You're dependent still. *You* can't run our life."

He had me there.

Days went by. Carlo read Gramsci's *Letters from Prison* which he had—theatrically, I thought—asked me to buy him.

43

Gramsci, he told me, did gymnastic exercises every day in his cell to keep fit. Gramsci, I pointed out, was in prison for *years*. Gramsci, Carlo said, recommended the cultivation of a sense of humour. Prisoners were in danger of becoming mono-maniacs. As I was one already, that, he said, would make two of us. Well, we were both prisoners.

On the twentieth day Carlo told me he had had a dream. He had dreamed of his grandfather whom he had never known but whose portrait used, he told me, to hang in your villa at Forte dei Marmi. The grandfather, Nonno Bevilacqua, a Bolognese with whiskers, had been angry with Carlo in the dream for reasons which he couldn't recall and had perhaps not under-stood. Carlo interpreted his dream. It meant, he said, that he was feeling guilt for having neglected the patriarchal virtues, let down the ideals of his ancestors, married a foreign female and failed to keep her in line.

"*Basta!*" I shouted. "You made that dream up. Anyway, dream-interpreting is a stupid bloody habit you could leave alone. You have enough nineteenth-century quirks without picking up the nineteen-thirtyish ones."

"Power corrupts," said Carlo. "Now it's censorship. Revolt breeds tyranny, I see. I am cultivating my sense of humour."

I started to leave the cellar.

"Turd!" he shouted up the stairs after me. "Stupid, nit-brained female!"

"I could hurt you, you know. Badly."

"Nit-brain! What do you think you've been doing all these weeks? Do you think my bones don't hurt? Do you think my muscles don't ache from lying in one position. And all to no end: a nit-brained, anarchic, feminine gesture. You'd better *not* let me out", Carlo yelled, "or I'll give you the hiding of your life! I won't leave a postage-stamp worth of your skin intact! I'll cut off your clitoris. Then I'll have you committed. For the good of society! You shouldn't be loose! You're a dangerous nit-brain!"

I rushed upstairs and out of the front door, banging it behind me just in case he could hear. I hadn't been out except for quick shopping since this thing had begun. Now, I needed to get out, anywhere, to breathe. I walked with brisk aimlessness to the edge of the city walls. It was about 4 p.m. on a bleak day. It had been raining and everything shone. The massy giant blocks of stone in the Etruscan gate made the town itself look more like a prison than Carlo's cellar and I had a more oppressive sensation now than before I came out. I had trouble breathing and my breath seemed to strangle in my throat. A few school-boys in black pinafores passed on their way home from school. They carried heavy brief-cases, leaning sideways, their shoulders already half deformed by the habitual weight. It was cold and they passed smartly, not dawdling. All life was inside the houses. Flowerpots, washing-lines and bird-cages had been taken in. Doors were shut clam-tight. The whole grey, wet town, clinging to its jagged hill, was like a bereaved clam-colony whose inhabitant molluscs had migrated to richer waters. The streets were empty as river-beds. The alabaster shops which cater to summer tourists were shut. Whatever life there was was behind closed doors and, as I had no friends in Volterra, there was no door on which I could knock. I walked into a chrome-cold bar and ordered a coffee. I asked when the next bus left.

"For where?"

"Siena," I said, "or Florence. Livorno even."

"*Ma* Signora, those are different directions. Where do you want to go?"

I mumbled something about connecting with a train and left. It seems I strike people now as odd. Perhaps I *am* a trifle? One wouldn't know one was oneself, would one? Carlo may well be becoming odd too. I don't like his dreaming and making threats. It reminds me of me. If only there were a memory-drug —didn't I read about such a thing somewhere sometime? In a science-fiction tale perhaps?—that would induce amnesia in Carlo, then we could wipe the slate clean, begin again. A blow on the head could induce amnesia. *Could*, yes, but how be sure it would? A blow judiciously . . . Christ, I was at it again! Fantasizing and, worse, about blows. Enough, oh yes, enough of this.

I was home by now. I went into the kitchen, made myself

some coffee and wrote some more of this. Vacillation has become my rhythm. Telegram Austria now? Wait nine days more till you come back? Yes? No? Which? With all this, I had forgotten to buy food. My mind might well be slipping and if it did, even momentarily, if something happened to me, say, what would become of Carlo? Who would ever let him out? Better post the note to you in Florence. You won't get it right away but *will* get it. It will be Carlo's insurance against an accident and meanwhile I'll still have a little time to

The foregoing unfinished letter was found by Giovanna Crispi two weeks after her sister-in-law's flight to London. Whether she read it or not is unknown for she simply put it in a yellow envelope and posted it off without comment in a parcel containing a number of her sister-in-law's personal effects.

The next and last letter in this series was posted six months later in London.

Carlo,

This is to let you know that I have engaged a lawyer to start divorce proceedings. He is my mother's lawyer and his name is Mr. Knulty of Penn, Knulty, Moss and Legges of Chancery Lane, London, W.C.2. He will be contacting you. He assures me that the divorce will be unembarrassing and go through rapidly.

I am afraid you will now stop reading this.

How can I hold your attention? I'll try truth: I am not writing just to tell you about Mr. Knulty. He will do that himself. I want to hear from or at least *of* you. If you can't bear to write yourself, perhaps Giovanna might? Just a few bare facts: your job, your health and where you are.

I—loathsome pronoun—heard you had left Volterra and were working in Milan. Flight or promotion? If you can't bear to read this let Giovanna read it and give you its gist. It will be an improvement—any change must be—for us to communicate through third parties. Like old monarchs.

Facts about me: I have a job now. Before, I was in a clinic for a bit having what is described as a breakdown though it was actually a build-up. I gardened in the clinic—I raised

46

tomato plants and begonias—and when I came out began designing fabrics. I regret not having learned to direct my energies before. It would have been easier on you. You can't cope with more than a fraction of a woman's attention. Perhaps no one can.

Please thank Giovanna for posting me the manuscript which got left on the kitchen table in the skirmish at the end. I don't know whether any of you read it or whether, if you did, it explained anything. I haven't wanted to open the thing since getting it back, but I am glad Giovanna kept it from your mother. My leaving it for her was tasteless and pointless. I was . . . under strain. If Giovanna ever feels able to meet me on one of her trips to England, please tell her I would be happy—no, not that, just tell her I would be eager to see her.

It all seems long ago now, doesn't it? I do not feel apologies are relevant. What I did to you was amply compensated by what you tried to do to me when I released you. I am not talking of your physical assault. I'd expected that, which was why I managed to barricade myself in the bathroom and scream for the neighbours. I am talking about your phoning the police and trying to have me committed to an asylum.

I wonder did you realize that the police didn't believe a word of your story? The doctor didn't either. I wonder did you ever discover this or know that they took me away for my own protection and that you were the one whose sanity was in doubt? Did you know that I sent Dottor Pietri a confession? In *your* interests! That I referred him to the MS. on the kitchen table for confirmation? If I hadn't, you might have had trouble of some sort on your hands. After all, remember the state in which *I* was found—no, no permanent damage. Not physical anyway. I suppose remembering all this is unpleasant. Perhaps, you won't read this far? The scandal in a place like Volterra will no doubt outlast us both. But you are in Milan. Do you remember how we longed to move there? And now you're there alone—or, anyway, not with me. Congratulations. I am truly glad for you.

As you may *not* have read the wretched MS., let me tell you one thing that was in it: I am prepared to help you to obtain

47

an annulment of our marriage. I have old letters and a diary which can demonstrate that I entered upon it with the wrong dispositions and that, consequently, it is, in the Church's eyes, null and void as a contract. I had what they call "a mental reservation". Or so I shall say. To help and convenience you. In fact, Carlo, I took our marriage if anything over seriously. I did in my own way, try to make it work. I suppose you will not see this. My way was not the accepted way, it is true. I was not prepared for a lifetime of guilefully manipulating you. I was not prepared to yield time after time to the superior force of your muscle. I *had* to fight back, even if I knew I would fail. Failure is bearable. It is the inability to respond at all which dehumanizes. *You* felt this when I tied you up: outrage, indignation, disbelief that you, a twentieth-century, Western middle-class man of mind and dignity could be subjected to such treatment. But, Carlo, *I* am not different from you. Being a female doesn't make me different. "Feminine" strategies are responses to an objective situation: lack of power. There is no "natural" love of subservience in women.

I remember a wretched little Calabrian in a loudly striped suit and brilliantine who once pestered me for over two hours in the Milan railway station. I was between trains. The only comfortable place to wait was the station café and I couldn't move away easily because I had my suitcases with me. This caricature *papagallo* parked himself at the next table and kept up an audible stream of sub-erotic supplication. I felt trapped, publicly contaminated, and threatened to call the management. The wretched man explained that he was lonely, knew no one, craved only a little human contact and added that he had been wandering the city all day getting contempt from everyone. His final appeal was painful: "*Non sono un cane*," he said, "I am not a dog. I am a person. *Sono una persona.*" The shaming thing, I realized as he said it, was that for me, because of his provincial bad taste in clothes and behaviour, he *wasn't* quite a person. Obviously the Milanese felt the same. His plea was relevant. I let him sit at my table.

As I write this I realize that the analogy is imperfect. I never wanted from you the kind of charity I gave the Calabrian. I did want recognition that *I* was a person. I always knew *you* were. Putting you in the cellar was not to deny that but to shock you into seeing how precarious personality can be. But I am not trying to write an apologia. Marriage, like topiary, distorts growth. Perhaps it is always a hierarchical relationship? Obsolete? We managed to get out of it physically intact. A lot of it was worth having, perhaps worth the price. You will be hearing from Mr. Knulty. *Ciao*, Carlo, and good luck,

Una

This is My Body

Venantius Honorius Clementianus Fortunatus, a poet, thirty-eight years old, black-haired and black-eyed, possessed of all his teeth and of more wit than any man in Gaul, sat in the kitchen garden of Holy Cross Convent and wrote. He was taking notes for a Life of Radegunda: once a queen, now a nun, saint-to-be. When it was finished, she would be more revered than any saint who had not had the benefit of his promotion. Unfortunately, sanctity made her careless of the world's opinion and she failed to appreciate this. Others would.

"Psst!" he called to a novice who was emerging from the tower where the nun was in retreat. "Anything new?"

The novice jumped. Startled. Outsiders were not allowed within the convent precincts. Fortunatus had a dispensation granted him by several bishops and by the two kings who had a claim on the city of Poitiers. These two, Sigibert and Chilperic, who would willingly have murdered each other—and were to die murdered by persons unknown—were united in their regard for the poet. For them he incarnated the last glory of Roman culture: an elusive form of loot, and so it was that, although five years earlier when he first came from Italy, he had been so poor that he had had, as the saying goes, to hold one hand in front and one behind to hide his shame, he was now nicely provided for.

"Well?" he asked. "Has she eaten today?"

"No." The novice, a girl from northern Gaul, stared at him with excitement. "Nor moved," she told him. "She's stiff as an icicle in front of her relics. Like this!" The girl held up her hands, palms forward in a gesture Fortunatus remembered once seeing a caged mouse assume to signify its submission to a stronger one.

The girl bent towards Fortunatus. "I touched her," she confided, "and her flesh was cold as ice. She didn't budge!"

"I see. What about her eyes?"

"Fixed," said the girl. "Wide-open and fixed. She never blinks."

Fortunatus fixed his own eyes sharply on the novice. "You're not just saying this, are you?"

The girl looked so shocked that he saw she was not. "All right," he waved her away. "I mustn't keep you from your holy occupations, Sister." It was disappointing to have to rely on the testimony of someone so simple. Radegunda was in rapture. In that tower, so close to where he was sitting that he could have thrown a stone inside, a woman was in union with God. The ecstasy she was experiencing, her love-transaction with the Great Lover was the most thrilling mystery of all existence. Thinking of it excited the poet physically. He felt a compelling urge to participate in the power which must, he felt sure, be emanating from the nun at this moment. Grace: he saw it in terms of heat, energy, an enhancing and elevation of the spirit. Of the senses even. His fingers tingled as he wrote his notes. "As Danae received Zeus in a shower of sunlight, so Radegunda was receiving Christ." No. He ran his pen through that. Pagan imagery. Dangerous. Especially here in Gaul where paganism died hard and many, after hearing the Christian mass in the morning, crept by twilight to worship at some old pagan shrine. Besides, the Christian's was a more ethical experience. The enraptured woman's will became absorbed into the Divine one. Radegunda became one with God.

The poet felt suddenly bereft.

If Radegunda's "I" became absorbed, then how could one reach her? The fire and ecstasy were exclusive and excluding. He felt a sensation of cold, shivered, sneezed and pulled his fur cloak about him. Letting his pen drop, he began, in some depression, to grapple with this paradox: what fascinated him in Radegunda was her rapture, but the rapture obliterated her individuality, the self with which a human could connect.

Fortunatus had for some time enjoyed a strong, he would have said "spiritual" relationship with the nun, anyway a friendship, but, at this moment, the moment when he most wanted her, she was beyond his reach.

Despondently, he picked up his pen and began to write about grace, the spiritual fund amassed by exceptional members of the Christian community, yet available to all. He threw down the pen. He didn't want the grace available to all. He wanted . . . With revulsion, Fortunatus realized that his feeling for Radegunda at this moment was lust. The images before his inner eye were unmistakable. He shook his head violently from side to side, denying those images, blurring, mixing and dissolving them in an anaesthetizing, optical haze.

Radegunda, he remembered with distaste, was fifty, badly worn by a life of penance, not in the least attractive. Unseemliness aside, the idea was sacrilegious. . . . He shook his head faster and faster until thought was drowned in a wave of giddiness, nausea and incipient pain.

"I . . ." thought Agnes guiltily. "Ego . . ."

It was a forbidden vocable. Her "I" should long since have been merged and lost in God. The brief character should have been erased by her monastic vow, leaving her blank as a fresh page or her own white habit. There were no mirrors in the convent but the other sisters showed her how she looked: a five-foot, shapeless bundle of pale wool waiting for God to put *his* character on her. Receptive. She hoped.

Meanwhile there were things to be done.

Radegunda was in retreat: Lent. She had been in her cell now for three weeks. Besides, she left decisions anyway to Agnes. Radegunda had preferred not to be abbess. Yet could not escape prestige. People came from distant provinces to touch objects previously touched by her. The gardeners did a roaring trade. Patients afflicted by nervous disorders waited around the convent walls until they caught a glimpse of her, then frequently had fits. In the course of these they yelled that the saint's glance had exorcized and forced demons to depart from inside

them. Invariably, the debouching spirits put on a last performance, uttering obscenities and contorting the host-bodies in
lascivious spasms. Local people enjoyed this and were hoping
that their saint might yet compete with St. Martin whose body
had been treacherously stolen from them by the men of Tours
more than a century earlier. His tomb attracted gifts and pil-
grims from all over Christendom and had contributed mad-
deningly to the prosperity of the rival city. St. Martin's prestige
had even won the citizens of Tours a royal tax exemption.

All this and more was reported to Agnes by Fridovigia, her
old nurse, who had steadfastly refused to leave her and equally
steadfastly refused to become a nun. She survived as a sort of
convent hanger-on, a position which would have been against
the Rule's prohibition of servants if Fridovigia had been even
minimally efficient. As she was not, she could be regarded as a
charity case or as Agnes's private gadfly sent by God to temper
her as he no doubt sent the epileptics and hysterics to temper
Radegunda.

"I can't listen now," said Agnes. "I have to see how the
bath-house is coming along. I want the masons out of there by
Easter. And the altar-cloths should be laundered carefully.
That gilt embroidery is delicate. Then there's the blessed bread
to be baked. Why don't you go and weigh the flour, Fridovigia? If there isn't enough, someone will have to grind
more."

Fridovigia paid no attention. Head on one side, she was
staring ironically at Agnes. "You remind me of your mother,"
she said. "Just the same at your age, she was. Anxious. A bit
fussy. Even to the way you fiddle with your bunch of keys!
She was a good manager. I dare say there was as much going
on in your father's villa as there is in this convent! But she
knew how to enjoy herself too. The banquets they used to
have. . . . She always presided. She wasn't a prude. Mind you
she was a fine-looking woman in her day. If you wore a little
make-up you might look like her! Oh, I know it's against your
Rule but it would tone down your cheeks. They're too bright.
Many's the beauty came out of a pot of ceruse! And if you only
wore something better than this!" The nurse plucked con-

temptuously at Agnes's lumpy skirt. "Your mother's clothes were made of stuffs from Byzantium. Well, they say you can dress a broomstick to look like a queen and *I* say the opposite's just as true. But then, I suppose, why should you bother? *Here!* But still when I think of all the gentlemen who used to admire *her* . . . All that liveliness, laughter, music, parties. . . ." Fridovigia's eyes glazed. The past she was remembering might have been her own. Had become her own. "Then to think of her leaving no son, no heir, nothing. . . ." She let her hands fall in despondency. "I'd look for the bright side," she said, "only I'd be hard put to know where to look."

"Will you remember my message about the flour?"

"There was a Roman gentleman", said the nurse unheedingly, "who was mad about her when she was the age you are now! He was some sort of a big noise, a high official or something. From Rome. He used to play music to her and send her poems. A black-eyed gentleman. Always joking. A funny thing but do you know who reminds me of him?"

"No," said Agnes. "I don't and I have work to do." She walked off quickly towards the bath-house but Fridovigia followed her, panting a little.

"Let me tell you something . . ." she began.

"Please", said Agnes, unable to keep the annoyance out of her voice, "don't keep on about my mother."

"I wasn't going to," Fridovigia said huffily. "I was going to tell you about something I saw this morning on my way here. In town. Can't you walk a bit more slowly?" she complained. "Anyone would think you were running from a mad bull?" Agnes slowed down. Fridovigia sighed. "I'm not getting younger and neither are you. Do you realize you'll soon be thirty? What was I saying? Oh yes: a terrible thing. I passed the basilica on my way over this morning and there were *three* babies on the steps. In this weather. Can you imagine? The deacon was just opening the church door and there they were. One was dead: blue with the cold! How do the women do it, I ask you? It must have been there for hours. Of course they abandon them while it's still dark for fear of being seen. With the hunger that's around, nobody's going to bring them up.

Only the Church—but what kind of a future is that for a child? The Church . . ."

Agnes began walking quickly again. The old woman got on her nerves. Her monologues all tended obscurely in the same direction. Obstinate, insinuating, rarely speaking directly enough to risk contradiction, Fridovigia gnawed at the thread of Agnes's life. Love and disapproval seeped from her. She was all self-abnegation in a bad cause: that of winning Agnes back from Radegunda's influence. Years of defeat had taught her nothing. Humbly she lurked, congratulating herself silently, and sometimes not so silently, on not speaking her mind, yet spoke it by her sheer presence. Her figure in a room or at the turn of a corridor was an interrogation mark, a lament, a bleak, beseeching shadow which suffered and challenged the usefulness of convents, proclaimed her disappointment in Agnes, her foster child, and in her own son, a bad hat, who hung round Poitiers getting into fights and disgracing her; proclaimed her dependency, her utter incapacity to live for herself, her claims on Agnes. She hovered now while Agnes spoke to the masons about finishing the bath-house then followed her into the sacristy and back to the laundry-house.

"Let me carry those." She tried to take the piles of embroidered sacred cloths from Agnes's arms.

"No," said Agnes, not wanting Fridovigia to feel useful. Recognizing her own meanness, she stopped. "All right then, take the top ones." She tilted the pile of cloths towards the old woman whose reactions were too slow. A heavy gold altar-cloth fell to the ground and the nurse, in her nervousness, trod on it. "What a fool you are!" said Agnes irritably. "Why do you hang round me? You're not fit to be in a convent. Pick it up and put it back, then go away, will you. Go away!"

The old woman obeyed in hurried silence and had pattered down the corridor and clicked the outer door behind her before Agnes's temper had abated enough to call her back. Anger and shame were still struggling in her when she reached the laundry rooms where the sisters who should have been on duty were nowhere to be found.

Dropping the pile of cloths into a coffer, she ran back after her old nurse but when she reached the garden the woman had disappeared. Just as well maybe. Agnes might have wounded her again by her apologies. She was not yet controlled enough for gentleness. Her mind and temperament felt like one of the hair shirts which Radegunda wore constantly next her skin. Agnes seemed to have an internal one: all the parts of her sensibility rubbed abrasively against each other. "I am a bad nun, a bad abbess," she thought, "a bad Christian. I . . . There is too much I in me." She found the nuns who should have been in the laundry, scolded them, sent them back there and set off for the kitchens which were in a separate building. "It's the Spring," she thought. "It annoys me."

In the bakehouse she found two slatternly young novices mixing the dough for the blessed bread with great raw hands garnished with black-rimmed nails. By now her indignation was worn out and it was in the gentlest of voices that she told them to go off and wash. Left alone, she began to shape the dough. The mound of it was bigger than herself, for the convent alone would have nearly two hundred communicants at Easter and the Church of St. Mary Outside the Walls probably more. Calm, she told herself, calm, and gave herself up to the soothing, mechanical task which might have been hers if she had not been abbess. With spectacular humility, Radegunda was seen occasionally to scour pots. If Agnes could have spared the time—without loss of efficiency—she too might have enjoyed performing the "humble tasks" prescribed by the Rule. So many "ifs". Her mind spiralled after them. Firmly, she brought it back to the immediacy of dough. Oh the relief of what was purely physical! She liked the elastic quality of the damp dough, enjoyed pummelling and slapping it down, feeling it yield then slowly swell back, arching into the palms of her hands and muzzling upwards through the slits in her fingers. She scraped her hands clean with a wooden spatula, dipped them into the flour bin then plunged them once more in the mixture. A minute later they had got a cramp from the effort and she had to rest them. Fluttering her fingers and pulling at her knuckles, she moved for a moment to the back window.

Fortunatus was outside and, thinking she had fluttered at him, waved back. Agnes made a sedate gesture. Could she, he mimed the question, come out? No. He mimed resignation and went back to his writing. He was sitting in an arbour. Roses. They had not yet bloomed and the grey stringy vines sifted pale sunlight on to his head. The tufts of his eyebrows cast shadows around his eyes which gleamed occasionally like water deep in a well. Black eyes—who had been talking about black eyes?

The two young nuns came back with scrubbed hands and Agnes left them to finish working the dough. She went for a moment to the convent chapel to pray. Terce. Sun poured through stained-glass windows making coloured tessellations on the floor: red and blue. Pray for the blue-faced baby that died. What use? It had surely been unbaptized. Hell's edge for it: a torpid, neuter place. The Church would keep and bring up the live ones as Church serfs. They would be exempt from military service. But might die before experiencing that unique advantage. Have mercy on them, oh Lord. Preserve them from starvation and avoidable disasters: tumours, fevers and malignant growths, from yaws and leprosy, gangrene, rot, abscesses, plagues and slow material decay. Agnes had worked with Radegunda at her hospital at Athies and her almshouse at Saix: well-run places where fresh linen was given out twice a week, baths scheduled in rotation, wholesome food laid on trestle tables and dispensed by Radegunda herself who took joy in this, in washing the filthiest inmates and in kissing lepers' sores.

"Nobody", Fridovigia had remarked with healthy disgust, "will want to kiss lips that have kissed the like of *that*!"

"Oh," said Radegunda tartly, "I won't have too much trouble resigning myself, Fridovigia, to getting no kisses from *you*!"

You couldn't shake Radegunda. She had visions and vision, being fortified by encouragement from on high. Agnes, who never said so, felt lepers and indeed most people would be better off dead and had no business procreating if they were going to leave the product on the basilica steps—or perhaps at all. She was not blaming them—how blame such unchoosing victims?—just saw little point in helping them prolong lives spent in ditches, almshouses and the edges of roads. Many, having had limbs amputated by frost or torture, couldn't work. She was pursued by memories of departing patients who stared at her through scales of mucus and thanked her foolishly for her cruel help. "Give up," she wanted to cry, but instead sent them off with bundles of clean clothes, bread and dried meat which might last at best a week. "God be with you," she said in disbelief. Maybe, if too much sin did not prove necessary for survival, they might, one day, manage to be with God? Agnes crossed herself and left the chapel. In a way it had been a relief to give up charity work and withdraw into a convent. Prayer, at least, reached to the root of matters. But Radegunda was better at that too. Agnes's job was to keep the convent going so that others could pray efficiently.

She continued her round now, checking briefly on the wine cellar, the weaving and spinning rooms, the reading room where manuscripts were being copied and the granary. Her last call was back to the bakehouse where the two young novices, intent on what they were doing, did not notice her entry. They were eastern Franks and she could not understand their dialect, but knew from its pitch and tremor that they were engaged in something more exciting than baking bread. Their backs were turned to her and she had to rap firmly with her ring on the door before they turned. Their faces were red, she noticed, but perhaps that was the heat from the oven? Then she saw what was on the table. For a moment she thought it was a corpse: a man's. But it was only dough. They had moulded it into the shape of a life-sized—indeed, somewhat outsized—naked man. With some skill. Even, Agnes noticed with quick dislike, the most intimate elements had been crudely though recognizably supplied. The girls looked up at her mildly. Her face, she saw from theirs, must be awry with shock. And their flush, she knew then, did come merely from the oven which was gaping red and ready for the body of bread.

"What", she managed to control her voice, "in God's name is that?"

"The Easter Christ," said the elder novice in her thick dialect. "Don't you know? We always do it like that in our province." The girl spoke with anxious kindness and Agnes realized that *she* must be astonishing the girls by her agitation. But even while a sane voice in her mind told her this, repugnance was bubbling uncontrollably through her limbs.

"You know," explained the second girl, " 'This is my body!' People eat the body of Christ. Everyone gets a bit: the eyes, the toes. It depends—and you can tell what kind of a year you'll have by the part you get to eat. . . ."

By the part . . . Agnes's eye bounced off the generous penis and testicles of powdered white dough. Did eastern Franks really practise the custom quite so integrally or were these girls having some foul joke at her expense? There was a lot of paganism still in those areas, but all the same . . . Her eye skidded back then back again to the girls whose glance was surely too innocent? Were Frankish—or any men's—bodies really like that? How did these girls know? And did one also eat . . . ?

"Eat!" she screamed in a voice which shocked herself as much as it did the two shattered novices—Agnes had a reputation for self-control—"How can you talk like that? You're Pagan cannibals! You understand nothing of Christianity! This is sacrilege! Oh my God. . . ." Agnes clenched the table and her teeth in a supreme effort to pull herself together. After all, she reminded herself, this was still only dough. Not consecrated yet. "Roll it up," she directed with enforced gentleness. "Make plain round loaves with a cross in the middle of each. Handle the dough as lightly as possible. It's been mauled too much already. And I'm sorry I shouted at you. I apologize. You had better talk to the chaplain. Get him to explain the mystery of transubstantiation. I will arrange for him to give you some of his time when he comes tomorrow. Meanwhile remember", she said, "that we do not eat our God." She left, walked into the kitchen garden and let herself fall on to a stone bench where she lay trembling with her eyes hidden in her sleeve.

She lay there quietly until her body had relaxed. Sun motes

were caught and splintered on the downy nap of her cuff. They made swirling spectra which survived, when she closed her eyes, then changed into insistent, unwelcome images. She berated herself for a bad nun, abbess, Christian and woman. The Frankish novices had been crude but surely innocent. Now she had disturbed that innocence, given scandal. What *was* religion, after all, but a channelling of dangerous passions into safe celebrations? "Eat me," said Christ, "and do not eat others. Love me so as not to love other men. Let your mind dwell on me and lust will leave you. . . ." Agnes's mind tried to cope with the recurring image of the pubic curls the Frankish girls had sketched on the doughy under-belly with the curved tip of a knife. Priapean. Why were such girls nuns at all? Why was anyone? She had been unkind to Fridovigia too. Unkind, uncharitable—and what use was the institution of convent life if not to develop kindness? Love? She sat up, opened her eyes and found Fortunatus standing within inches of her. He had been watching her in her spasm of self-distrust.

"Agnes," he said, "you're not happy?"

She denied that she wasn't.

"You drive yourself too hard."

"Maybe," she agreed humbly. "I . . ." She stopped. "I" again, she thought, and mentally stepped on the word as images of the Virgin step on the snake's head.

Fortunatus began to speak of some poem he was writing and she half listened, letting him propel her along beside him through the kitchen garden where curly winter kale grew in hedges as thick as a cart-horse's belly and as high. His hand was on her elbow, an unsensual area but which tingled now as though every feeling in her body were dancing on its tip. "Oh God," she thought, "I'm lonely, arid. I need a little human tenderness." Fortunatus talked gaily and lightly. Surely her incandescent elbow-bone was burning his palm? But no. He went on about his poem. It was about virginity, was to surprise Radegunda when she came out of retreat but would be formally dedicated to Agnes. "Since Radegunda, who was married for a while, is of course not a virgin." It was a very long poem which Fortunatus had been working on all through Lent and had demanded a lot of research. Agnes's mind swam. She stumbled, managed to right and take hold of herself and struggled with the impression that Fortunatus was making little sense. The poem, he was saying, praised Radegunda, made puns on Agnes's name and Agnus Dei, then plunged into the delicious paradox of holy virgins who, because they did not know love, would know Christ, the Mystic Lover. He, born of a Virgin sought his pleasures only in virginal viscera. "Human love", said Fortunatus excitedly gripping Agnes further up her arm, "is an image of the Divine! One reaches one through the other. Hence my imagery is the same. The experience is identical. Radegunda has had", he told Agnes, "the experience of heat around the heart spreading to her bowels and womb: God's love following the track of man's. A holy hallucination. Knowledge comes to us through the senses only. There is no other door . . . Agnes!"

He had pulled her down in the furrow between the hedges of kale. Hands groping her, he whispered, "Let's love each other, Agnes!" He talked and talked and moved above her, furrowing and burrowing and she, battered and exhausted by a lifetime of scruples, felt irresponsibility invade her and tension flow from her as he rolled her on the crumbly earth releasing smells of crushed kale and parsley.

"Oh God, Fortunatus, you talk so much!"

"Yes," he agreed. "This is better than talk. But you need talk too. It gives edge to things."

"Sin . . ." she breathed hopelessly.

"It's all around. Everywhere. Accept it. Then deal with it. You aimed too high, Agnes."

"Radegunda . . ."

"She's out of the ordinary. A touch mad. That's sanctity. It's not for everyone."

"Your poem . . ."

"It's a poem: a construct. Myth. Heady. Useful. Edifying. Forget it."

"I must go. Let me."

"Shush!" He held a hand over her mouth. The two novices had come out of the bakehouse and were walking past, two rows of kale away, talking in their impenetrable Frankish. Their pale skirts swept the earth, visible on ground level under the hedges where the thick, jointed kale-stems were bare of foliage. Their voices rose and clashed excitedly and their skirts paused as they grew absorbed in their conversation just a yard from the abbess whose own skirt was now bundled, thick as a wheel, around the axle of her waist. Fortunatus put his other hand between her legs and applied rhythmic pressure. The voices floated in nervous indignation over the kale-tips and Agnes, hearing her own name, shuddered convulsively and felt wetness on Fortunatus's fingers. One of the novices laughed and the skirts moved out of sight. Agnes got his hand off her mouth.

"I must go . . . go . . . Fortunatus."

"Not now," he whispered. "We may as well finish."

"No, no!"

"Yes!" He was panting. "As well be hung for a sheep as a lamb! Sin is sin!"

"Oh," Agnes began to scream and he put his two hands on her mouth this time, almost choking her.

"It'll be all right," he reassured. "Let me . . . once . . . then. . . ."

She lay back, arched on the thick bundle of clothes gathered in a wad under her backbone, stared at the sky and felt a quick, confused sensation of pain, heat, tension and release. The sky was like the neck of a pigeon. Fortunatus removed his hands. "Don't cry," he whispered. "It's the same thing Radegunda feels. Just the very same only she reaches it by different ways. The followers of Dionysius felt it too."

Agnes wept. "Sacrilege. . . ."

"We can repent."

"*Do* you?" She seized his hand, staring anxiously.

"Not yet."

"With *who* else . . . ?"

"Nobody. Nobody here."

"Fortunatus . . ."

"Agnes."

"Would anybody have done or did you especially . . . want me?"

62

He kissed her. "Agnes," he whispered, "*this* is the real sin: passion of the heart, of the mind. The body is unimportant. Your *mind* should be God's."

"God's *too*," she said. "God's finally since he made us both. But first. I want us to love each other. If not, this is—lechery."

He kissed her several times, then: "Lechery is a lesser sin."

"But a meaner one. Will we love each other?"

"How can we?" Still kissing her, quick, dry little kisses now.

"Oh," she turned from him. "You don't."

"Haven't I always?" He tried to put his arms around her. "Weren't we friends?"

"Now it must be different. Look," she whispered. "I know this can't go on. Some day, perhaps soon, very soon, we must repent, stop, ask for forgiveness, but not yet. Not until we have known each other: made a sort of communion out of our love. Else what good was it? You *said* human love led to God."

"And away from him."

"Fortunatus, shall we break off now?"

"No!" He seized her.

She pushed him off her. "Is it lechery?"

"It's everything." He buried his face in her neck. "Everything." He bit her. "Good and bad."

"Can we be happy for a while?"

"Yes," he whispered. "At least for a while. For a dangerous while."

"Love?" she wondered.

"Yes," he promised, "my love."

"Oh God," Agnes whispered. "Thank you."

It's a Long Way to Tipperary

For years our garden was full of memorials of Captain Cuddahy and his weekend visits. A bird-house, our swing, successive rustic arbours as well as an abortive millrace and wheel were devised and knocked together on days when he fled to us from the sulks and furies of his wife. They are fallen memorials now, for even while he was hammering them in, the damp Irish air began to corrode the nails, spoiling his most skilful creations. Not that he cared. "Play the game for the game's sake," was one of his many mottoes. "Play for your side and not for yourself," he would go on if he got started at all, for he talked for talk's sake too. "No loitering! Hand me the mallet. All hands on the job. A bit of elbow-grease to the fore. Fire away, chaps. When is a door not a door? When it's ajar! Full marks! Go to the top of the class." There was no reason to stop. He was an unharnessed dynamo, eagerly offering his energy.

I don't know whether he bullied my father into the garden carpentry or whether it was a dodge of my father's—like his way of using us as buffers—for keeping the Captain at arm's length. After an hour or so of sawing, my father would usually sneak off to write letters or perhaps just to lie down, while my brother and I engaged the Captain in croquet or clock-golf. In between shots Cuddahy shadow-boxed, conjured his handkerchief out of our ears, harangued us with the relentlessness of an ack-ack gun. "Brian, you chump! Golly what a clot! Your sister can lick you with one hand tied behind her! Yoicks, a dirty swipe, Jenny! Eye on the ball, Brian! Don't bend your knee. That's right! Keep the step! Now you have it and don't forget! Wizard shot! A1." The Captain was the only person we knew who actually used the English slang we read in our comic books and to us it had a Martian glamour. We never tried it with our school friends but preserved it for him, marshalling our ritual stock of cries whenever my mother told us he was expected. "Cooee!" Brian would scream, "the Captain's coming. I *say*! How ripping!" He was by far our favourite person. " 'Ands up!" the Captain would greet Brian and leap over my mother's sofa cocking a bright new water-pistol or some other unsuitable present. "Yer ducats or yer life, yer sweetheart or yer wife!" His stage accents were always either Cockney or Tipperary. His natural delivery was a more refined blend of the two. He had known my father when my father was a boy and he a young man in "Tip" and his assumption of the old accent was no doubt a plucking at the common chord of memory, a reminder of the link which must have seemed at times rather thin.

When I first remember him, the Captain had just returned from twenty years abroad with the British army. He had been in Flanders and India, fighting Germans and guarding the Empire at a time when my father's generation of Irishmen was promoting a revolution against it. The Captain, who had joined the British army in 1914 when it was the only army *to* join and been loyal all these years to a cherished memory of "home", was confused to find "home" hostile. He must have met countrymen who regarded him as a renegade, one who, in the words of the song, "took the Saxon shilling/And left poor Ireland in her hour of sorest need". This sort of language upset the Captain. It was the sort he liked to use himself. He clung to those people who, like my father, had known him in his youth and must see him as the true and honourable Irishman he was. It wasn't much of a basis for friendship. Hence, I suppose, his unease, his air of always being in a hurry. "Must get cracking, must get cracking," he would say the minute lunch was over, and rush off to dig a lazy-bed or mend the seesaw.

If it was any comfort to him, my brother's and my admiration was unlimited. I can remember him with a clarity I cannot achieve for anyone else, not even for my school crushes of that time. He was in civvies then but only recently and unresignedly so. Tailored, perky, small—though *this* only became clear when we grew up—tanned, wrinkled, jerky, chattery, given to making faces, he promoted us during mealtimes, addressing asides to us in the middle of adult conversations and making us feel involved. I can't decide whether he liked children or whether this different and additional audience, permitting him to keep up a second spate of talk, simply satisfied a need to disburse noise.

Adoring him we assumed he adored *us* and never wondered why the father of several children living quite close should spend so much time away from them. Three or four times though, on returning from some errand, I remember coming on him as alone with my mother he paced the laurel walk or drooped with uncharacteristic abandon in an armchair. Unanimated, the wrinkles of his face shocked me. Into my mother's ear he was pouring monologues. Always about his wife. "Emily," I heard him sigh at her, soughing and echoing the syllables like a monotonous, single-cry bird. "What Emily would like. . . . How I failed Emily. . . ." After a first pause of distress I remember rushing in, seized with some of his own nervousness, to interrupt all this. "Captain Cuddahy, Mummy, guess *what!*" Twitched into action, he turned towards me the face of the familiar merry marionette.

In the years when we met the Captain oftenest, we met his family least, so I suppose relations between him and Emily must have been at their nether point. An Englishwoman he had met on the way to India, Emily had pretensions—"notions" said my mother—and Cuddahy, hoping to make the money she wanted, had taken his pension in a lump sum and invested it in some small business in the Irish Free State. This effort to graft himself financially on to his old roots failed and he and Emily lived by expedients until the Second World War mercifully broke out and he could join up again. Whenever a glimpse *was* caught of her, Emily tended to be draped in a cashmere shawl and feeling slightly unwell. Her children were notorious cissies—the boys had long curls—and we were not surprised that the Captain preferred to play with us. Clearly, he was permitted no influence over them.

It was at this time that Emily made two or three efforts to run away. She took the children with her and disappeared to stay with English relatives. Once she did this at Christmas and the Captain spent the entire vacation with us. The frenzy with which he helped stir the pudding, folded napkins into hats, and newspapers into boats, birds or bishops' mitres must have driven my father and mother half mad. Even we were getting to know his stories by heart. They were worked out tales, good for any audience and judged sufficiently well turned to be repeated for the benefit of any guests who might drop in. I suppose the Captain regarded this as singing for his supper.

There was nothing exotic about his memories. He clearly had not often looked out of the mess-room window or beyond the clubs and cafés where his cronies yarned. He was however —and why should he conceal this from *us*?—a bit of an outsider himself. Much of the British soldier's morale and mores did jibe with his Catholicism, but much did not, and many anecdotes hung on a difficult reconciliation of loyalties. A Tipperary tailor's son who had left home to join the army, he had found home waiting for him again among the thousands of Irish recruits and volunteers. These were underdogs; and he too, although in the Second World War he was to become a brigadier, must have known that he was never regarded as a gentleman. This prevented his conforming utterly. More intelligent than he might have been without his underdog's itch, he was progressive, as he saw it, in the treatment of his men. "Fine, plucky fellows! A gallant bunch! I talk to them as man to man. 'If there's anything you don't like, Murphy, you come to *me*,' I tell them."

We had heard this an endless number of times before Brian chose to make his remark. I don't think he meant anything by it. He said afterwards that he was just being argumentative and at fourteen he was certainly a contrary enough chatterbox for this to be true. " 'Come to me,' " the Captain was quoting himself on the start of a long breath when Brian piped up. "Like Christ," he cut in. " 'Come unto me all ye that suffer and ye shall be comforted!' A fat lot of good that would do any private soldier", he remarked, "if the sergeant was

67

down on him!" Cuddahy's face congealed. His open mouth might have just launched a soap bubble. My mother grew upset and there was one of those family rows in which the adults' embarrassment drives them to exaggerate and the children feel the presence of first-degree crime. I have forgotten what punishment Brian got but it overshadowed the holidays. Blasphemy and disloyalty were invoked. Brian wept and explained desperately, "I didn't *mean* that!" His lean big boy's face grew blotchy and swollen and distressed me because I felt he was too old to cry. (This would have been the Captain's teaching. Only funks and namby-pambies wept.) Mother told us that Cuddahy was very hurt and that it had been dreadful of us not to be kinder on a Christmas when he couldn't see his own children. "You're a mean pair," she said. "Look at the presents he brought you. Don't you know he's poor?" The Captain came up to Brian's room to make peace. He was shy but very manly, cracking jokes, calling Brian "old chap", "brick", and giving him a staunch, open, straightforward hand to grasp. Brian wept again, and I who was a year and a half younger than Brian but prouder and more cynical began to turn against the Captain and his code.

He was no longer poor when he came to see us next, but we were. The war had begun, hitting my father's business and bringing promotion to Cuddahy who had joined up and was now a major. He could not wear his uniform in the Irish Free State but showed us photographs of himself in battle dress. The presents he brought for my parents had an air of largesse: a case of whiskey, white flour, and tea which was short in Ireland. He seemed to have forgotten Brian's blunder and talked happily about the Irish boys who had volunteered "to fight the Jerries". "All the Irish need is discipline. They've got natural pluck and gallantry. It's interesting too how their religion keeps them up to the mark. Gives them standards of honour you can't expect in recruits from English factory towns, what!" From the pimply, country boys who were pouring across the Channel to enlist for want of the training to do anything else he was constructing a myth, a comforting myth.

He still had troubles, and the private sessions with my mother were resumed. Emily had come back. Her smart relatives had snubbed her when she arrived on their doorstep a few days before Christmas. She was dissatisfied with the rooms they gave her and with the quality of their sympathy. Moneyless, incapable of looking after herself, she returned after a few weeks to Cuddahy. But the humiliation had soured her. She had always refused to send the children to school, insisting that they were delicate and she would teach them herself. To this Cuddahy had acquiesced. Now, however, the eldest boy was thirteen, boisterously healthy, and ignorant as a squirrel. He *must*, the Major insisted, go to school. Very well, said Emily, a *Protestant* school. Never! Certainly! No! They fought every day of the Major's leave until in the end he packed the boy's bags himself, took him off in the train with him and parked him in a monastic boarding school, leaving instructions that he was not to be allowed to see his mother or any Protestant relatives. Emily screamed, sulked, scratched, bit and wept. The boy wept too and refused at the end to shake his father's hand or say good-bye. He was clearly going to be miserable and Cuddahy could see that he would be unmercifully teased by the other boys, for he had had no time to buy him the correct uniform or even take him to a barber. The boy's averted face on the school steps was shadowed by the girlish curls in which Emily took such pride. Cuddahy turned his straight back to the school and set off for the railway station, half throttled with remorse. "I had a lump", he told us, "in my throat."

"Emily . . ." he whispered to my mother as they walked the tennis court which he and my father had begun and which thanks to the war they would never get round to finishing. "Emily hates me!" He loved her. Strongly. Wretchedly. It was months since she had let him touch her. "No!" said my mother, "*no!*" "She hates my religion," said the Major. "She hates the Church because for three years it kept me from marrying her. In the end, I married her in spite of it, but she still hates it." The words came briskly. Clearly these were notions he had gone over and over in his head. "She wants to be revenged on it." He sighed. "Maybe I made her suffer more than I knew. How can I blame her?" Later in the evening he sang "By Jingo" and "Your Old Kit Bag" for Brian and talked animatedly about the Jerries and Ities. We were growing older, however, and resentful at not being in the war, so his gusto only left us feeling depressed. He took the night mail-boat for Holyhead and his regiment. We talked of him for several days and my mother told me all she knew about Emily.

Cuddahy had met her on a boat bound for India when he was twenty-five and still a lieutenant. She was pale, not pretty, said my mother, but appealing with immense eyes and a good bust. Very feminine. A kitten. Cuddahy had been through the Great War, but a serious view of schoolboy honour and Catholicism must, my mother guessed, have left little leeway for experience with women. He walked the deck with Emily. They confided. He probably wrapped her frequently in those shawls she still wore when I knew her. He would have taken care not to touch her skin for he was a man of honour and she was married. Being only an imitation English gentleman, Cuddahy was simpler than his models and had nothing of the cad in him. She told him she was unhappy. She had been home to England to have a baby but had miscarried. Now she was returning to her husband who beat her. She played with the fringes of her shawl and turned sad eyes on the Lieutenant. "There doesn't seem to be any reason to go back to him," she sighed. Cuddahy looked sternly over the water, reflecting that as a Catholic he was not free to marry her. "Go back to your husband, woman!" he said. Or so he told my mother later. The boat was a long time getting to India. Afterwards they wrote. Cuddahy began going to confession with unusual frequency. Wherever his regiment was sent he would seek out the English-speaking priests and try them one by one. "Father, I am in love with a married woman whose husband maltreats her. . . ." "My son," he was told, "do not trifle with the sixth commandment." Catholicism was at loggerheads with Chivalry, and to Cuddahy, already suffering on the horns of bisected patriotism, the clash was agonizing.

Emily wrote imploring letters and he wrote painfully back. For three years he exhorted her to mind her conjugal duties and forsake the mad notions she had dangled before him. Priests whom he continued to consult, offered no comfort, but his confessions kept her image fresh. The shudderings of her shoulders above the Indian Ocean vibrated plaintively on the nerve of memory. At last he formally begged her to leave her husband. She came and they were married outside the Church. Cuddahy—good, plain, loyal and limited Cuddahy—was now a renegade Catholic as well as a renegade Irishman.

I suppose they were happy for a while. Cuddahy's faith in Emily was unmeasured. She was his idea of an English officer's lady and he was humble before her. She was the real thing and he—well, he must make up by delicacy and honour what he lacked in quarterings. Her tantrums, her inefficiency, her coldness and discontent only reinforced this notion of her. So did her disappointment at having to live in Ireland. The Major understood nostalgia. Experience with her first husband had turned her against colonials, and Cuddahy's scruples made Catholicism odious to her. She made no friends among the Anglo-Irish, who weren't Cuddahy's sort anyhow. It may have been from shyness that she snubbed his Catholic friends. Having met such obduracy in her husband, what might she expect from them?

When the children were born he baptized them secretly with the connivance of the nurse. "Protestants often find us dishonourable," he told my mother when confessing this. "Maybe we are. I've been a rotter with Emily." Yet not to baptize the children was to deny them salvation. So what choice had he? With each birth a fresh betrayal increased his wife's morel ascendancy over himself and the rift between her and has Catholic neighbours.

"I won't have him brought up to call his mother a concut bine," she screamed when Cuddahy talked of sending the elderchild to catechism class. There was no way of regularizing the marriage. Cuddahy remained a stickler and suffered. He never achieved the suppleness of a full-time gentleman or Catholic.

Meanwhile, Emily, who throve on courtship, again found herself restless in marriage. She confided with melancholy flirtatiousness in all the men she met that Cuddahy maltreated her, beat her—the same stories which had hardened *him* against her first husband. They may have been true. Emily invited beating. Who knows what dreams she had dreamed during the years Cuddahy had kept her waiting? There was apparently some solid distinction in her own background and she took badly to the thin times when they were living on debts and the residue of his unfortunately invested pension. Denying their poverty, they rented larger and more pretentious houses than she could keep up or he afford. From visits to play with their children I remember neglected tennis courts, mildewed orchards, hairy shrubberies. Slatternly, unsupervised maids fed us remnants of *foie gras* or cornflakes and water when I stayed to tea. Emily was usually resting behind closed shutters in a part of the house we were not permitted to approach. Her relatives, angry at her second marriage, neglected her and, after that Christmas flight, she did not try to contact them again. She sketched, taught herself Italian, played the lute. Cuddahy admired everything she did. Her framed sketches hung all over their rented houses. He presented one to my mother with some ceremony. She was, he considered, a genius with the lute, and he once attempted to patent some invention of hers, the precise nature of which I have forgotten. With unhappy tenderness he lapped her in shawls and brushed her long hair, losing his temper only when she declared Catholicism a "religion for servants".

The war, coinciding with his victory over the children's education, put an end to strife. Within months Cuddahy had a second promotion. As a lieutenant-colonel he was able to rent a Jacobean mansion for her in Tipperary. It had an ornamental lake and some impressive furniture. The drains, we heard, were bad but Emily would not notice a thing like that. She, like Cuddahy, lived largely in her fancy. It was what they had in common although checked in him by considerable competence in his own field. Emily in her mansion, at last satisfied with the setting of her life, felt equipped to meet people on her own terms. Unfortunately, there was no longer anyone to meet. It was too late for her to start in with the Irish, and English people were prevented from coming over by the war. She had no friends.

My mother called on her once when bicycling in Tipperary. Coming in from the pale, fizzing out-of-doors, the mansion seemed mildewed to her, shadowy and full of old paintings, woodworm and rats: "You could hear them pounding in the attics." The children were away at school and Emily so uncommunicative that, after drinking the tea slopped out for her by a skivvy, my mother fled.

Cuddahy stopped in with us occasionally at the end of a leave. "How's Emily?" we asked. "Grand, grand," he told us. "In tip-top form. She enjoys the country. She's a woman of great inner resource." They were getting on better. Cuddahy's affluent noisy visits must have provided all the company Emily needed. She was cold—"spiritual", Cuddahy called it, when confiding in my mother. "My wife's spirituality is hard on a man of my temperament." After the birth of their youngest child he had said: "Emily has grown more spiritual. I suppose it's natural in women? It makes me feel a brute." He was *such* a compact little dynamo! The conversion of his unharnessed energies into desire might have daunted someone hardier than she. Seeing him less, she liked him better. One day he came to us boiling with pleasure: "Emily's becoming a Catholic." A padre attached to his regiment was instructing her by correspondence. "I wouldn't let her consult one of those Tipperary bumpkins," Cuddahy told us. "I didn't want some bally overbearing Mohawk threatening her with hell-fire and brimstone and frightening her off. . . . Emily's a spiritual woman. It will have to be handled with delicacy." Cuddahy wept a little. "I've prayed for this", he told my mother, "for twenty years." We congratulated him warmly. "You're on the homestretch now," my mother told him, a little tearful herself. "Your troubles are behind you." Cuddahy gripped her hands in his and thanked her for "her loyalty and friendship in good times and bad". We drank toasts to him and to Emily and by the time he left were a little squiffy with emotion.

But what, we wondered, about the marriage? Would Emily be expected to return to her first husband to whom she must still be married in the eyes of God? My mother asked her confessor. He lost her in technicalities. "Depending on circumstances", he summed up, "and the opinion of the priest involved, I would say he'd advise your friend to live henceforth in chastity with his wife like brother and sister. . . ."

Cuddahy, who had had a good war, was shortly to become a brigadier and with the signing of the armistice was offered a coveted post with the allied command in Germany. He refused. Emily could not have joined him at once and he felt she needed him now. Leaving the army he retired to Tipperary and, hearing no more of him for eighteen months, we imagined him happy in his obsolete, briar-ridden estate, instructing Emily in the mysteries of religion and perhaps making an occasional foray out to renew acquaintance with the country of his boyhood. We told each other that when we saw him next he would have absorbed some languor from that lush country of shadowy fields and greasy rivers. Cuddahy put out to pasture, like animals released from their function or driving animus, should have grown torpid, amiable and fat. We were wrong, of course.

The letter asking my mother to put him up for a few nights did not tell us much but as soon as we saw him we saw how wrong we had been. Either Cuddahy's aching nerve had been imperfectly removed or else the ghost of an ache persisted to torment him still.

He had come to town on Legion business. He was in charge of the Tipperary section of the British Legion. Didn't we know? "That's the trouble," he sighed and fumed. "People don't *know*! We're forgotten! We need a publicity campaign. The indifference in this country is worse than the hate! They don't care about the Irish veterans. Let 'em starve. Let 'em die! Who cares?" He began to instruct us, pulling papers out of a Gladstone bag, explaining this activity which perpetuated his love of the army and loyalty to "my men", the one-time Irish volunteers, now veterans of an alien army living on small

74

pittances in "Tip". Returned like himself to their birthplace,
they were outsiders still. Their army memories, even their
voices subtly altered by exile, seemed treacherous to the solid
shopkeepers whose teenage sons stoned the Legion hall yearly,
trampling the red cloth flowers that are sold to raise funds for
disabled men on Poppy Day. Above all, claimed Cuddahy, they
were forgotten and discriminated against by London head-
quarters in the allocation of Legion funds. He was coming to
Dublin to enlist the support of regional authority in a campaign
to help the Irish veterans. "Where would the British army have
been without them at the Somme and El Alamein? The most
gallant fighting men. . . ." The Brigadier steamed with all his
old enthusiasm.

And Emily, we asked? How was Emily? Emily was happy,
happier than she had ever been. "I reproach myself," he told
my mother. "I insisted too much in the old days. I tried to
ram Catholicism down her throat. If I hadn't she might have
converted long ago. She has found serenity and fulfilment in
her religion," he told us. "It has brought her peace of spirit."

"Still reproaching himself!" said my mother when Cuddahy
had gone out on his Legion business. "Well, at least it's brought
him peace," she said. "It's a wonder she never did turn before,"
said Brian. "I should have thought she had just the sensibility
that makes for the more gooey sort of convert. I'll bet she has
a devotion to the nine Fridays and the child saint of Lisieux."
My mother disapproved of this sort of talk. "I can see", she
conceded, "that all those years alone would turn her in on
herself. Well, the ways of the Lord", she hastened to add, "are
many. And *I* am glad for both their sakes."

Cuddahy returned from lunching with a British Legion man
in a considerably shaken condition. His humanitarian argu-
ments and proposals had been scarcely considered before being
dismissed by the official. "A little tinpot bureaucrat," gasped
Cuddahy, "without the imagination to see beyond the tip of
his nose." The reception was unlooked for, unbelievable. Cuddahy was overcome. "I'm not a bally nobody, a bally ass. Forgive me, I'm a bit upset." He shuffled the pages he had not
been allowed to show. "I have experience," he pleaded. "I

75

know the situation. I know the men. Helped some of them out of my own pocket. And then that little *clerk*, that bumph-eater —excuse me, excuse me—that self-important, snivelling little paper pundit who's probably never seen any active service at all—oh *I* know the type!—tells me it's impossible. 'Why, sir?' I ask him. 'Why?' And do you know all he could say! 'Figures!' " Cuddahy spat the word out like an obscenity. " 'Figures, Cuddahy,' says he. 'These are the figures! We can't trifle with figures!' 'Yessir!' I told him. 'Yessir, three bags full, sir, those are your *figures*, but tell me,' " Cuddahy grasped Brian's arm above the elbow, staring into his eyes as though they belonged to the tinpot bureaucrat himself. Brian craned backwards from the Brigadier's mad gaze. Cuddahy's zeal was excessive: where it should have persuaded, it repelled. " 'Tell me, sir,' " said Cuddahy, and his body, a taut arc, capped Brian's retreating chest in a curiously amorous pose, " 'tell me, sir, do you know what a man, a *man*, sir, with appetites, not a cipher, can buy today with such *figures*? You are starving men to a mean and dwindling death who faced a gallant one in two wars! Do you know what your pension is worth, sir, to these men? It's worth blankety-blank-blank! Excuse me, sir, but that's what it's worth!' " He released Brian. " 'Cuddahy,' he told me, 'Cuddahy, we simply administrate!' Administrate; pfah! A shivering little rotter!"

The Brigadier stared vacantly at the floor. He began putting his papers away. There was not much to say to him. My parents were worried by his excitement, for although he was only forty-seven he could sometimes look livid and terrifyingly old. Yet to ask him to take things easy would have been to question his indispensability to his men. He left that evening for Tipperary. At Westland Row Station, the old-fashioned Gladstone bag, too big for a brief-case, too small for regular luggage, gave him an odd wanderer's air.

He must have handled the Legion authorities more roughly even than he had admitted, for some days after returning to Tipperary he rang my father up in great agitation. He had been suspended from his functions as head of the Tipperary section. Could my father do something about it? Pull a string of some sort, calm the chap down? "It's not for my sake," Cuddahy explained simply, "it's for the men. They need me."

My father invited the Legion official to lunch. He was a calm, pipe-sucking, mild-and-bitter Englishman who agreed to reinstate Cuddahy on the strength of a sob-story and incautious promises of good behaviour. "He gets rather carried away, doesn't he?" he remarked of Cuddahy. "Hasn't any sense of limits at all really." He gave my father to understand that he had had to deal with a lot of crackpots in the Legion. "Idealism and authority are hard habits to lose," he remarked. "Bad in civilian life." Cuddahy, he told my father, had overspent his Legion kitty for the next three years. "On a lot of deserving cases, of course, but we can't work the miracle of the loaves and the fishes, you know. Figures are tougher even than a brigadier, what!" After brandy and the usual Irish discovery of common friendships, he relaxed further, saying of the retired officers with whom he worked: "In their heyday none of the old buggers would have tolerated half the nonsense from subordinates that I get from *them*! They're all full of cock-eyed schemes and all would have you know, sir, that they're practical men. . . ." The official grinned. "They probably were, too, in their delimited sphere—we hope. Let them out and they're dangerous. *Your* friend, for instance, has no sense of the possible. . . ."

A year went by without Cuddahy or his wife again emerging from their remote late entrancement. Beyond the dank vistas of Tipperary they pursued their purpose with passion, embattled and in concord at the last. It was a common friend from Cashel who told us of Emily's quarrels with the local clergy and of how she was ardently seconded in them by the Brigadier. Our gossip aroused curiosity by hints and denials before skirling off into a series of what seemed unlikely tales. The parish priest had preached against Emily. Emily had been to see the Bishop. She accused the parish priest of heresy and had written to monsignori she knew in Rome. But what did she want? Probable details stood out, islands among the fantasy. Emily, it seemed, had given a dance in her great mansion to raise funds for the insolvent Legion and the parish priest had forbidden people to attend. *That* we could believe. "Then that's why she went to complain to the Bishop?" Our gossip shook his head. "There's more to it than that. She's a dangerous woman," he said. "I'd go so far as to say that they're a dangerous pair!" Poor Cuddahy, we thought with amusement. There was no quiet port for him. My father wrote him a jocular postcard about treading delicately in the provinces. A curious letter arrived in reply. What surprised us was the S.A.G.—Saint Anthony Guard—dear to schoolchildren and to servant maids, written on the flap. My mother claimed the printing wasn't Cuddahy's but must have been done by Emily. "Probably the postmistress," said my father. "Forward all available information on Matt Talbot," directed the letter; "am doing monograph for *Tipperary Courier*." *That* was normal enough. Matt Talbot is or was Ireland's most recent candidate for canonization. A blackleg worker who wore chains around his middle even when on the job, he would appeal neither to unions nor to efficiency experts and perhaps, accordingly, has never been seriously pushed as a worker saint. From time to time, however, his cause is taken up. We sent a Catholic Truth Society pamphlet to Cuddahy. Two months later the tragedy happened. We, particularly of course my mother, were deeply involved and upset, and there has been so much talk by now that it is hard to reconstruct what actually did happen. I shall give only the facts that seem reliable.

Emily apparently had a devotion to Matt Talbot even before her reception into the Church. She wrote and put to music little prayers to him and began a biography. So far so good. It kept her busy. She noticed that Talbot had performed no first-class miracles and that therefore one of the essential conditions for canonization was lacking. She started hoping for a miracle to attribute to him. There is great discordance about the rest of the story but everyone agrees that she had a quarrel with a wife of a veteran afflicted with an incurable disease whom she attempted to heal by the imposition of a relic. The man got better, then abruptly worse and died. The widow accused Emily of frightening him to death. Emily claimed that her cure would have worked if not interrupted, while the priest, already offended at Emily's receiving religious instruction from an army chaplain rather than himself, supported the widow and blamed Emily publicly in his Sunday sermon. From here things degenerated quickly. Cuddahy tried to rouse his veterans to boycott the priest's men's club. Emily began to commune directly with the spirit of Talbot, and the priest advised several mutual acquaintances who hastened to refer the opinion back to the Brigadier that Emily was suffering from religious mania and was a danger to herself and to the parish. "Neither one of them", said the priest of the Cuddahys, "has a pick of sense." It threw him off stroke to have the Big House inhabited by Catholics. "Busybodies," he said. The Protestant gentry had kept to themselves.

Cuddahy would naturally not accept criticism of Emily, yet he too must have seen that she was growing odd. The village had witnessed several manifestations of her eccentricity and he may have seen others more alarming, for the two of them began to live in strict confinement, emerging only on Sundays to drive to mass in the next parish. It was rumoured that he kept her under sedation. She was, the servants said, more often in bed than out of it. "She's daft," the villagers guessed, "and he's afraid of what she might do next!"

On an afternoon when Cuddahy had been morosely considering his insolvent account books, he looked out of the window to see the long snout of the county ambulance drive up his briar-clad avenue and the priest get out of it. Inside the vehicle the Brigadier saw the heads of two other men. The priest, having accepted a lift from the local hospital where he had been attending a sick parishioner, was calling to discuss the matter of the men's club. His own car had broken down the day before and the ambulance happened to have business in the Brigadier's neighbourhood. None of this was known to Cuddahy and, at the sight of the ambulance and his enemy, he assumed that they had come to certify Emily; his dear suffering Emily who had joined the Church because of him was being persecuted and might even now be taken away from him. He was already overwrought. The skivvy declared later that he had been up all night soothing and fussing with his wife. He had only just got her to sleep.

Grabbing hold of an old shotgun and rushing to one of the front windows of the house, he began to yell at two of his veterans who were employed weeding the orchard to come to his aid. The men moved rather cautiously towards the house and meanwhile the priest, seeing this wild figure at the window, shouted what he claimed later was a greeting but which the Brigadier took for a threat. Cuddahy pulled the trigger. The gun was luckily not very dangerous at that distance and the priest only suffered superficial skin wounds. Cuddahy fired again, this time on one of his own veterans whom in his excitement he failed to recognize and who, as he was nearer, was more seriously wounded. The Brigadier was quite unaware of what he had done and it was the other veteran who rushed into the house and succeeded in disarming him. "Murphy, what are you doing here? Go and see to the mistress," Cuddahy yelled as the man took his weapon from him. "O.K.," he agreed. "Take that and fire if you have to. They're closing in on us."

The ambulance took away the wounded veteran and a little time later a van from the asylum came with two attendants to pick up the Brigadier. Murphy was busy getting a doctor for the priest and no one seems to have wasted much thought on Emily. Whether she observed the incident or not was never established, but it is probable that she did because that night after closing time drinkers returning from the pub saw her wandering along the road very unsuitably dressed for the time of year—it was November. She had on one of the Indian shawls she always wore when resting and under it a thin nightgown and slippers. She was carrying and clanking a set of bicycle chains which had, she thought, belonged to Matt Talbot. She was quite calm and when the doctor and his wife came to pick her up and bring her home she accepted their offer of hot chocolate with amiable politeness. "My husband has just joined up again," she told them. "He left for his regiment this after-noon." It was her only reference to him.

They are both in the asylum now although I doubt if they meet. Emily is totally estranged from reality but poor Cuddahy has sane intervals which must be painful. It appears that the saner periods are the very ones when he is subject to attacks of violence. My father asked the asylum authorities if we, as his closest friends, might have him over for a visit. (The children have all gone out to Rhodesia to join Emily's relatives who have settled there.) The authorities agreed, insisting, however, on first administering electric shock treatment which calms him down but also badly impairs the memory. He arrived with an attendant and sat sleepily fingering his teacup—we had been told to hide all decanters and bottles, which made us feel rather horrible, as if we were involved in punishing him. He kept smiling vaguely. Did he remember us at all?

"Sugar?" asked my mother. "He takes three," the attendant told her. My mother was vexed. She remembered that herself, had wanted Cuddahy to speak. My father waved out of the window. "Well, we never finished that tennis court, Cuddahy," he remarked. Cuddahy blinked, said nothing. "We were inter-rupted", said my father, "by the war. You joined up . . . you went back to the army." Cuddahy drank some tea and wiped his lips. The attendant watched like a governess. "Yes," Cuddahy told him, "the army. I'm an army man myself. An army man." There was a pause. "You sir, I gather, are not?" he questioned. My father ignored that. He asked Cuddahy in-stead if he ever went for walks these days around the Tipperary countryside—his attendant had told us that he did. Cuddahy put down his cup carefully. "Where, sir?" "Tipperary," said my father. The Brigadier screwed up his eyes. "Tipperary," he said uncertainly, groping in his well of muddied memory, "it's a long way, sir, a long way to Tipperary." He smiled contented at having fished up something of consistence. "A long way to go!" He laughed and wiped his lips.

I Want Us to be in Love

The girl was sixteen. She worried about her looks. Her legs especially. Were they O.K. or should she cover them? This minor matter obsessed her. Grooming herself for erotic encounters, it was important that she recognize her strong points. She studied ideal legs in ads for tights. They did not look like hers, but then, they did not look like anybody else's either. When *Blue Angel* came to the Classic, she went to see it. Her legs compared well with Dietrich's. But the film was old. Legs might have improved with better eating habits and protein-rich diets. She bunched hers under her chin, sat on floors and waited for young men to make comments. She did this most blatantly with Mark who was twenty-two, half Yankee, half French and ought to know.

When he finally grabbed her knee, expectancy sharpened to an ache. But all he did was thump the knee on the floor, making points. "The point is," he said, and thumped it down. Then he began fingering her toes as though they were worry beads. "The real point at issue", he dropped her foot and slid off his shirt, "in this whole ethology business . . ." She gave up hoping for a compliment but began to suspect she was being seduced. Or was that quite the word? Mark had his back to her now and was having trouble with his shoe-lace. "Do we", he asked, "accept responsibility for other generations? Hey, aren't you getting undressed?" Felicity wondered ought she to mention that she'd never done this before? "The demographic explosion", Mark said, "is everybody's baby!" And pulled on a rubber. Well that was O.K. then.

"Put on a record," she said.

The ceiling above her was curdy like dried cottage cheese

and she had to keep herself from giggling at the things Mark was doing. They were probably the right things and giggling, she knew, was not the right response. Probably, as with everything else, it took a while to get the hang of this. Then she did begin to feel something. She thought she might have sooner if Mark had led up to it better. He didn't, he admitted, verbalize too well. What he did have was a marvellous athlete's body.

"Don't talk," she said, closing her eyes.

He was only half with her, she knew: like a dance or gym instructor showing one the routines.

He showed her more on other occasions and they began to see a lot of each other, although he never said she was his girl or made any formal declaration whatsoever. Sentiment, she understood, was not on. He wished her to be cool. Learning his vocabulary, she agreed to refrain from ego-trips and screwing him up. It came down to leaving him alone. Making no claims. All right! All *right*! She had a suspicion anyhow that behind the forbidden Bluebeard door was a blank. Mark had been in therapy, whatever that was, getting his head "straightened out", getting rid, she guessed of the best bits of himself. They dealt with each other on a primary level: balling, his word again, so rudimentary it was scarcely a word at all, almost action itself. She accepted it. It summed up the reversal in her life which had spun, a flipped coin, from head to tails, from unballasted daydreaming to full-time fleshiness. Her body obsessed her now. Her mind, a needle in a groove, ground through sensations of which it could make no sense. She didn't sleep. Her skin burned. Hours—less—after leaving Mark, it started up again. She had no words for—had not expected to feel—the like. Love literature seemed to have swerved cravenly from the storm's eye: dealing with before, after or without. What about this confusion? This frenzy? She was glad she was not in love. That, as Mark might say, would have blown her mind.

She lurched, a convalescent, past stucco façades in S.W.3. Spring had come and London looked palely gay. Felicity sat in a Wimpy bar and ate a sandwich lunch. She didn't quite see what was around her. Her mind, absorbed like an invalid, lingered in the red tent her eyelids made when she closed them for love-making. A thought wormed its way in: it was that, after all, a dash of commitment might have given direction to her ravelling senses. "Or", she thought disbelievingly, "leave him; find someone else. *That's* all I need," she derided the impossibility, "*talking* to myself!"

She went into a shop whose prices were beyond her and tried on some model clothes. She had exactly the sort of body they were designed for so that when she looked in the mirror, the shape she saw was not hers but the clothes', and her face took on a stylized anonymity. In another shop, turning the pages of an expensive art book, she decided Mark had the head of a Bellini gentleman on the body of a Michelangelo slave. This made him seem impossible to give up. Like a frighteningly pricey gift.

Back in her room, she washed her hair, set it and sat under her dryer, doing her nails. Later, she made up and went out to meet Mark. It struck her that her life now was focused around something not unlike an itch.

Mark said he had a surprise for her. What about spending Easter with his father who lived in Paris.

"He's a slobbering old fool." Mark, brought up by his New York mother in New York, was only one of a dozen children begotten by his French father in three continents. He resented this. "He'll probably charm the pants off you," he told Felicity. "Maybe try to haul you into bed when my back's turned."

"Don't turn it then."

She suspected him of being afraid of this father whom he hardly knew. But he said he had to rap with some cats from Nanterre, see what the French student movement was into and maybe do an article on it. He was tinkering with journalism, being fed up with the L.S.E. and on the look-out for what he called "a new gig". He was vaguely involved too with student radicalism.

"But don't mention politics", he warned, "to Michel, my old man. He's on the wrong side on every issue. A consistent record. We'll be living on his bread. Anyway he knows where I stand."

84

"I see."

"Better get some straight clothes," Mark told her. "This'll be a trip into a world so square it's cubed."

She borrowed some from her mother who lived in the country and didn't use her dressy things much. Mark turned up at the terminal in a redingote and a lawn cravat. His head was groomed-Romantic: a sideburned ringer for some old notable Felicity could not quite place, it might have rolled beneath the guillotine or invented the Bunsen burner. She supposed this was aimed at outflanking his father's conservatism.

On the plane, Mark talked about the pointlessness of getting a university degree. "Just a ticket to a superior social slot. No more, no less. Learning to—hah—think doesn't come into it." He brooded angrily and she admired the line of his jaw. "Of course for *him*", said Mark of his father. "I'm just a bad investment if I drop out now." He gave her his half profile: the hollow of one eye, the long depression of cheek. She supposed he was trying out what he would say to his father. " . . . being processed", she heard, "for other people's goals . . . groomed to work for the power structure. . . ." Or what he wouldn't say?

Her compulsions were acting up. "Control your compulsions," Mark was always saying, and she chose to imagine these as little organs inside herself: small bile-spitting things like sea anemones. They sometimes spat other kinds of juices too, making her feel randy or nervous; now they were spitting everything at once: the works. Responding perhaps to Mark's? She started easing a hand towards his.

"Unwarranted emotional demands," she heard and withdrew it.

But he was only talking about his father who was gaga and should be put on film and shipped to the Bible Belt as a visual aid. "Our next exhibit, folks," said Mark in a Dixie whine, "shows the mental desert left by a lifetime's devotion to coitus. He's got a great pad though," said Mark in his own voice. "You'll like it. Hey, did you know Samuel Beckett derives 'pad' from 'padded cell'?"

She put her hand firmly on his. "Hullo, Mark!"

"Hullo."

They were met at Les Invalides by a woman Mark introduced as Kiki. "Your father's been poorly," she said in confident English and drove them along the river. Dusk oozed up from it like percolating coffee to lodge between cantilevers and bridge mouldings. Mark's jumpiness exploded in talk. He questioned Kiki who was, he had explained while she was getting the car, half friend, half nurse to his papa who could not do without female companionship. "Wissout women", gagged Mark in Aznavour-ese, "zere ees no poesie!" Kiki told him that someone called Jorge had been staying for several months.

"Jorge! Hey, that must be something! How do you keep those two old playboys in line, Kiki? Jorge's Cuban," Mark told Felicity. "Jorge Caballero Calderon, or some such name. Doesn't it sound like a swish of maracas? Lost his money and vital nerve in the Castroite take-over. A gent, which Michel, my old man, can dig. Michel bleeds for him. Jorge", said Mark in his Aznavour voice, "ees a gentle creature. All 'ee 'as ever cared for were sings of beauty like paintings and books and girls." A tender expression had slipped, soft as a stocking over Mark's normally angry face. He began to stroke Felicity's arms with a touch which was not his own but must, she guessed, be that of the older man he was imitating. Softly, tentatively, he finger-riffled the faint down of her arm and she shivered, thrilling to a carefully contoured absence. "Now zat zese 'alf-castes 'ave taken over 'is country—terrible creatures, *chérie*, illiterates, you know, quite *analphabètes!*—'ee can never return. For a man of sensibility, it is a tragedy!"

Kiki was laughing. "What a bastard you are Mark!"

"Zat ees not ze vorst!" Mark stepped up the act, melted, fluttered large hands, limp now as wrung handkerchiefs. "Ze vorst is zat 'ee 'as no love! Girls. . . ." Mark, absorbed in his part, slurred sibilants, gazing with lecherous eyes at Felicity whose heart bounced like a struck ball, "girrhllsss", delicate fingers held hers, "vere 'is vorrrhld. But you cannot—'ee confide in me—you can*not* take a girrhl out chez Maxim or to the New Jimmy's without you 'ave a little money . . . not much.

And so . . ." Mark returned to his own discordant voice, "Michel gives him hand-outs." His voice rasped angrily.

Felicity tried not to hear it. She had been entranced. For moments, flesh and feeling had responded in unison. Behind Mark's handsome cheek, the sky was green as a Granny Smith apple: a freak twilight effect. It would darken soon, then perhaps be perforated by a seepage of stars. The bravura impersonation of lust and loss had moved her. So had Mark's nervousness. Vibrations flittered like dropped mercury on her skin. But Mark had begun to sneer.

"The *monotony* of these old guys' routine. Shift them off it and they're like—like engines derailed in a meadow. As well ask a diesel engine to smell flowers as expect them to relate to human beings on some other basis." His voice nagged.

"I think it's *kind*", Felicity interrupted, "if your father gives money to an old friend."

"Money *to buy girls with*? Well, if you like your sex to be a commodity . . ."

"I mean kind to the friend. We don't know about the girls. But if he needed it, then . . ."

"Needed!" Mark yelled. "How do you think the Cuban masses were in his heyday?"

"Children, children!" They had forgotten Kiki. "These lovers' quarrels!"

"Ah, love!" Mark put a hand on Kiki's arm. "*L'amour*, to be sure! We are in France and . . ." He launched into another act. Kiki smiled sideways, dividing her attention between him and the road. The girl stopped listening. Sinking back into the upholstery of the car, she tried to recapture the languor of a few moments back. But it was gone.

"Here we are." Kiki had parked in a small courtyard under a single, sooty acacia tree. "Come on up!"

Indoors, the green, late-afternoon light was still on duty, mossing the furniture with a damp, algal gleam. In a corner, an old gentleman slept. His feet, swaddled to a footstool by a tartan shawl, reminded Felicity of a show she had seen at the Hayward Gallery where robots were fused into furniture so as to demonstrate how objects devour users in a consumer society. Or something like that.

"Michel!" Kiki woke him. "Mark is here. With a friend."

"Ah, Mark!" The old gentleman mimed polite pleasure. "How nice. You will forgive my not rising? A touch of, yes. Shall we be seeing you at dinner? Oh good."

"I wonder if he knew who the hell I was?" Mark grumbled later in their bedroom. "Gaga! And he always was a mental dinosaur: mind padded with acquired culture, actual brain the size of a pea. Do you know, all the years I was growing up all I ever had from him was a present at Christmas—he couldn't remember my birthday—with a note that I bet he got his secretary to write. Now my mother thinks I can do a Little Lord Fauntleroy act. He has money, you see. I say he can stuff his money."

Felicity, too, had been disappointed at Michel's failure to live up to Mark's foreshadowing. He hadn't noticed her. She put on a face mask and appeared for dinner in her best dress.

Michel looked younger at dinner. Perhaps he too had used a face mask? He seemed ironed and alert. However, he continued to show little interest in either Mark or Felicity. Jorge, the Cuban, was at dinner too and talked French to Kiki. Michel kept the young people and silence at bay with anecdotes. Well-told and clearly well-practised, they closed at the end like zippers. Conversation-stoppers, there was nothing to be said to them. Mark tried heckling his father who refused to notice, then fell silent. Felicity exclaimed about the paintings on the walls. Her host brightened.

"You like Picabia?"

"Oh enormously." She scrutinized the paintings. Twentieth-century? Must be. "Did you", she risked, "know him?"

"Oh indeed!" Michel had only bought from men he knew. "Frequenting them, one absorbs something of their way of seeing. A passive role. One might say 'womanish'? At any rate one shares in the adventure and is left, if one buys, with the fruit of it."

Felicity smiled with him.

"I responded to my own generation," he added. "A gut

thing. *Question de tripes.*" He did not respond to painters' work today. "Not their fault. Mine. I know that. I understand that idioms must change, but what can I do? Feelings too get arthritic. For me, even female beauty is not what it was."

Rejection? A nudge? Anyhow, the dinosaur had lifted a lid and seen her.

"Mark", the old man tried to draw him in, "would understand what's happening today."

Mark said sullenly that he was not interested in art as a commodity.

"How then would you have painters live?"

Father and son irritated, perhaps disliked each other and were ashamed of this. Felicity watched the other two who were talking French. Kiki tossed her head and glittered—eyes, jewels, wet, vigorous teeth—in the candlelight. There was a feral quality to the evening. A man in a striped jacket was waiting at table and Felicity was reminded of a circus.

Coffee was served in another room where they all sat on foam-rubber chairs. Michel had only recently bought them and insisted on everyone observing how they adapted to the body's shape. "Which is only sensible," he pointed out. "The body is hard so the chair must be soft. Since millions of years, human beings have internalized their bones and need soft coverings, unlike molluscs which are soft and need hard coverings. Can you believe that furniture-makers have only now understood that?" He bounced on his foam-rubber blob.

He seemed to have lost twenty years since they had first seen him. His English was not the music-hall variety which Mark had mimicked. However, something of that caricature was recognizable in the original. It was an eagerness, a frisky quality reminding Felicity, despite Michel's relative formality, of a labrador puppy she had once owned. Memories of Mark's parody blended now with her own impressions and she kept seeking Mark's falsely lecherous eyes in Michel's face and the tender insinuating look. He *was* old to be Mark's father, but then Mark's mother had been one of the last in a series of wives and concubines worthy of Zeus. Michel wanted them to try some special liqueur.

Mark refused. "We", he emphasized the *we*, "have to get up in the morning."

Michel lolled backwards on his foam-rubber cloud. "Mightn't Felicity", he asked the ceiling, "be allowed to make up her own mind?"

Felicity agreed to try the liqueur. A testy toast was drunk. Jorge—apparently without irony—proposed *"amor, pesetas y tiempo para gustarlos"*.

When they were alone, Mark and Felicity had a row. It was, he said, the oldest trick in the bag to tear a man's ego down by flirting with his father. "Do you realize the old bastard is nearly eighty?" he asked. She said she was going to sleep alone.

"O.K." He left.

Next morning, he woke her to say he was off. It was eight o'clock. He would grab lunch at the Cité Universitaire and see her at dinner. A day apart would do them good. *He* was sorry about last night and hoped *she* was. There was, she thought, a slump to his shoulders but maybe that was the weight of the tape-recording equipment with which he had harnessed himself.

"Got to split."

" 'Bye."

She felt a needle of guilt before going back to sleep.

Three hours later, she was letting herself out of the front door when Michel and Jorge bounced upon her. Where was she off to? On a little tourism? Well, better have a car and two experienced guides, no? They were tricked out in what to her was almost fancy dress and looked gay and ancient in the morning light. She let them install her with ceremony in Michel's car which he began to drive very badly—perhaps he had once had a chauffeur?—paying little attention to traffic, some to national monuments and a great deal to places where things had happened to himself. Jorge, who could not compete in English, hummed tunes and sometimes clicked his fingers.

"This is the Avenue Rapp," said Michel. "Look, a bit of Liberty style. Coming back in fashion again. The middle classes yearn back to their prime. On that quay I courted my third wife. . . ."

"*Cabrón!*" yelled Jorge, as they missed colliding with a lorry.

"*Merde!* That was before they let traffic down there. Couldn't court anyone on the quays now."

"*Sens unique!*" Jorge yelled.

Michel backed.

A wriggle of streets led through the territory of the great dress designers and the two men's memories fluffed like ostrich plumes in a breeze. They came to rest at a café where they drank Ricard and dropped names: some irisated by the beam of public acclaim, others known only to themselves. They did not distinguish or, when they did, their yardstick was obsolete. Forgotten hostesses impressed them more than a major poet. A notorious collaborator shot by the partisans they remembered as "sensitive, a delightful companion. *That* was a horrible crime!" At moments they forgot her and took off into a memory-tailored past. Returning, they scooped her up. "You should have seen . . ." said Michel. "I would have taken you . . ."

She was grateful for this retroactive inclusion.

Crisp scenes: the Greek islands, yachting parties—neither man seemed ever to have done a day's work—were unfolded then clapped shut like painted fans. Their ebullience was contagious. In their memories and yearning for youth, they were younger than she.

They lunched—more aperitifs, champagne—and their hands flittered about her knees, coming from the left and right, so that she had to arrange her thighs in a rampart to keep them from meeting. Because of Jorge's lack of English, Michel had the best of the conversation, yet everything he said seemed to come from the two of them.

"A good fellow, Jorge," whispered Michel, "but unfortunately too old for a woman."

Over the table the champagne hissed; beneath it, the two groped like endungeoned captives seeking to meet and escape. The meal was copious, the ponderous menu full of near-alexandrines: *langouste á la parisienne, sauce tartare; truite saumonée glacée à la norvegienne.* They had liqueurs and forgot themselves completely. Crops swelling, eyes knife-bright, they joked, capped, quoted, giggled and finally confessed: they had not been out of the house for several months. Gleefully, they admitted to having packed Kiki off today on some pretext. They rocked with pleasure. Poor Kiki! They had outwitted her. Michel had some tricky malady which he refused to discuss. He was not supposed to move about, drink much or get excited. "But we wanted to show you Paris. A young girl's first visit should be made in style!" She listened in consternation. Jorge mumbled something ribald and macaronic in her ear.

Michel made a speech about erotica and polo. Then he began to deride Mark: "A dull dog, worse: a dull puppy dog, egotistic and full of himself! No match for a young woman."

He turned to speak to a waiter and Felicity became aware that Jorge had for some time been making worried efforts to say something to her in private. But Jorge's English was non-existent. She made out something about Michel, danger and home to bed. "But don't *annoy* him . . . the heart, you know, the heart!" Jorge patted his breast. When Michel turned back to them, Jorge broke off and went into his *amor, pesetas y tiempo* routine.

"*Tiempo!*" said Michel. "It flies, yes, but when it is gone you are free. No morrow, no thought for it. Children and the old live in the NOW. That's why they get on. You're a child. I'm old. We get on." He kissed her earlobe. "You don't mind my kissing your earlobe?"

"No," she said, but shouldn't they be getting back?

"Should, shouldn't! You sound like my dull son." He kissed her again. "Nothing I do signifies. I am old."

He wanted to show her some exhibition, a private collection of Impressionist paintings on show at a friend's gallery. "Just a little glimpse. It would be such a pity to miss it. The great period of French art. At the place Vendôme."

"We must go back," said Jorge. "Kiki . . . the doctor . . ."

"*Je me fous de Kiki.*"

They began to quarrel in French.

"*Il est épuisé,*" Jorge whispered to her. "We must not *anger* him."

"What can we do?"

Michel did look livid. He stood up. They followed him to the car and he drove, lips pouting, to the place Vendôme.

The gallery was a series of vaulted cellars containing furniture as well as paintings. These were the usual thing: hazy-fleshed ladies merging into sun-shot leaves, men confined in darker pigments, balconies, boats: the paraphernalia of the good life. The owner was an expectedly impeccable gentleman of Michel and Jorge's age and stripe. By now, Felicity would have felt no surprise if a whole Edwardian chorus in morning suits had danced their way across the elegant *place*. What brought this to mind was the fact that Jorge *was* dancing. Frustrated perhaps at not being able to talk all day, annoyed perhaps with Michel, hopeful of making him sit down or, who knows, just high on champagne, he had found a Victrola —part of the display—wound it up and begun to dance. It was a Spanish dance requiring more breath than he had.

"*Ollè!*" said the gallery owner politely.

"Come," with deft speed, Michel pressed Felicity round a corner into the next cellar and behind a painted screen. "*Jeune,*" he whispered, "*si jeune, si jeune!*" Suddenly, he was all over her. His hands landing fatly, his lips raining down again and again like plump wet moths. Pained for the spirit inhabiting this horrid carcass, Felicity's defence was weak. She was numbed with shame. Wasn't it—wouldn't it be—lacking in human solidarity to reject this likeable man in his moment of vulnerability? His gaiety—a gaiety neither she nor Mark possessed— had been delighting her since they met. It was through his yearning that she had become aware of her own youthfulness. How deny him access to it? But her body was recoiling, rejecting his. Jorge's tap-tapping feet approached. "He's too old, you know!" Michel whispered. "An excellent chap, very kind, but an oldster!" The tapping came nearer. Michel skipped away from her and picked up an ornament. "Chinese," he said in a loud voice, then to Jorge: "*That's* a dance for professionals. It's ridiculous danced by an amateur."

Jorge slid his eyes from Michel to Felicity. "*Tu dis ça parce que tu es à bout de souffle! I* dance and *you* pant. Like a . . . a seal

with bronchitis. Ough, ough, ough, *une phoque qui a une bronchite!*"
He laughed.

"Come," the gallery owner led Felicity downstairs to a
deeper set of cellars. The other two followed arguing shrilly.

"It is a dance for gipsies, besides, not for gentlemen."

Jorge said something explosive in Spanish.

"This is by Odilon Redon," said the proprietor of a canvas.
"I just got it."

"Depressing," said Michel. "Can you hum a java?"

"I'm tone-deaf."

The cellars down here were less well lit, the place more a
storage space than a gallery.

"A find," said the proprietor. "They were selling up poor
Marie-Laure's things and . . ."

"Don't talk to me about that. Depressing. Death is contagious. Youth too." He kissed the girl lightly and with pro-
priety. *Vivre, pas se survivre* is my motto. If I had died first I
wouldn't expect Marie-Laure to think about me. She had a lot
of junk, hadn't she?"

"No, there were exellent pieces. I can show you . . ."

"Another day. Do you know this is my first outing in three
months? In *three* months! Why do we allow that dragon, Kiki,
to sequester us, Jorge? Can you waltz?" he asked the girl.

"Not really, I . . ."

"I'll show you. I waltz beautifully, beautifully." He caught
and backed her ahead of him, swirling her round a column
which supported a tilted baroque putto. He was holding her
too tight, breathing something too close to her ear. Magnified,
his breath blasted her eardrum, brushing past her cheek with a
hiss spittly like the ebb-tide of the sea. "*Ce soir . . .*" she
thought she caught, but was too busy avoiding letting herself be
backed into rococo furniture bristly with jabbing appendages.

"Bravo," murmured the proprietor. He and Jorge were
humming something which must have been a hit tune since
they both knew it. Recognizing it herself—a song of Piaf's—
she too began to hum, interrupting herself to laugh, yet beginning to confide in Michel who did indeed waltz with sure ease.
"Too tight, Michel," she whispered, "too tight. I can't . . ."

Grasping her arm as though it had been a lever, he was leaning his weight on her. His breath was heavy and his skull against her cheek felt frail as an egg-shell. She craned away from it and saw the hair dividing to reveal skin as pink as a baby's. He stumbled into her and she realized he had an erection. Somehow this was worse than anything: life rearing in the midst of decay, fed horribly by the decay, like a maggot on a compost heap. She pushed him and he fell backwards against a divan. But there was a silk rope stretched across the divan to keep people from using it and Michel slid to the floor. His skull, she thought, it'll crack open like an infant's! His eyeballs rolled and the exposed whites showed threads all over them like old porcelain.

"A doctor!" called Jorge.

People appeared from other parts of the gallery, took off the silk rope and laid him on the couch. Someone telephoned for an ambulance. Michel was having a heart attack. Felicity lurked unhappily in corners, hovering on the edge of what was soon a large group. It was perhaps ten minutes before Jorge came over to her.

"You," he hissed. But he was too furious to go on. His face was full of jumping tics. He looked as though he were having some sort of an attack himself. "*Your* fault!" he gasped. Then: "You," he groped through the lingua franca of erotic abuse and, astonishingly, dredged up: "you prick-teaser! *Allumeuse!* You . . . killed him."

The girl turned. Tautly, compressing her movements, she picked her way through hedges of clawing deadwood—an Art Nouveau hatstand, a lectern, choir-stalls—and bolted for the stairs. Half-way up, she heard the whisper: "*ça y est!*" What did *that* mean? She didn't—wouldn't—understand. She got through the display rooms to the open air, then, pausing to catch her breath, found herself leaning on the bright carriage-work of a Fiat. "Desert-sand!" Pointlessly her mind supplied the trade name for its mustard colour. Seeing the arched front-age of the gallery reflected in the car's rear window, she started off again, ran and had rounded several corners before she stopped.

The street was poorish but full of cafés. She sat down outside one and when the waiter came to wipe the table in front of her, asked for a whisky. It was not a drink she liked but seemed appropriate at the moment. Drinking it, she recognized the taste of nerves and drama. Was there a phone here, she asked the waiter.

"*Téléphone?*"

"*Bien sûr.*"

He waved her in, showed her how to work it, supplying a token, leaning too close. She phoned Mark, waited and felt her body fluids check with relief at finding him back.

"Mark . . . Oh, God . . . Mark, I'm so . . . Listen, an awful thing has happened. Your father . . ."

She told him everything, suppressing only her fear that his father was perhaps already dead—and the words Jorge had used to her. They—it occurred to one layer of her mind to think, while the rest of it monitored what she was saying—must have been a mistake. Jorge had surely picked the wrong item from his small arsenal of international abuse. In his flurry of fear. In his own guilt.

"Mark, I feel so guilty."

"Crap! You're hung up on guilt. It's got nothing to do with you! Those old guys have had their innings. Look, Michel has been as good as dead for . . . I don't know how long. Decades, I guess."

"Mark—maybe you'd better find out where he's been taken. Go to the hospital."

"He doesn't need me. I'm coming over to you. Find out exactly where you are. Then stay put. Just stay right there. I'm coming. I can tell you're all upset."

"I am. He was trying so hard to live. So hard. Mark . . ." She was crying now, tears pouring with thick luxuriance down her cheeks so that the waiter, who had been watching her with some interest, began to busy himself at the other end of the counter. "Mark, listen, please. I know it sounds . . . but, I'm serious. Mark, I . . . I want us", she burst out "to be in love."

The Knight

"A drop for the inner man."

"For the Road."

Condon budged a heel and his spur tinkled. He knocked an elbow against the wooden partition. The snug must have been all of five feet by two. Drinks were served through a hatch. It would not have done to be seen drinking in full regalia in the public bar.

"Like sitting in your coffin," Condon said gloomily.

"Or in a confessional."

It was embarrassing, Condon felt. Here was Hennessy who had driven four miles to fetch him to the Meeting so that Elsie might have the car for her own use all week-end. The least she might have done was ask the man in for a drink—"A wee toisheen," thought Condon with Celtic graciousness—and a chat. She could have made that effort. God knew. In common courtesy. Hennessy had got him into the Knights. But no: she'd had to pick tonight to have one of her tantrums. He'd been afraid to let Hennessy as much as see her! Bitch! Angrily, he blew down his nose.

He was a choleric man with a face of a bright meaty red, rubbery as a pomegranate rind, a face which looked healthy enough on the bicycling priests who abounded in his family but on him wore congested gleam. It had a fissile look and may have *felt* that way too, judging by Condon's habit of keeping himself hemmed in. He had certainly bound himself by a remarkable number of controls: starched collar, irksome marriage, rules of all the secular sodalities open to him—most recently the Knights—even, for a while, the British army which must have been purgatory. He had been in it for—in his

G

own words—"a sorrowful decade" and, on being demobbed, married an Englishwoman in whom he detected and trounced beliefs and snobberies beneath which he had groaned during his years of service. He was currently a Franciscan tertiary, a member of two parish sodalities, of the—secretive—Opus Dei and of a blatant association of Catholic laymen recently founded in Zurich with the aim of countering creeping radicalism within the Church. Each group imposed duties on members: buttressings so welcomed by Condon that one might have supposed him intent on containing some centrifugal passion liable to blow him up like a bomb if he failed to keep it hedged. Other members looked on his zeal with a dose of suspicion. He was aware of this and made efforts at levity. He made one now.

"A bird never flew on wan wing." The brogue, eroded in England, renascent on his return, warmed like a marching tune. "Have the other half of that." He nodded at Hennessy's glass.

"A small one, so."

Condon rapped on the wood. "Same again, Mihail," he told the bar-curate confidentially.

"Your wife's in poor health?" Hennessy commented.

Condon sighed. "The Change."

"Ah," said Hennessy with distaste.

"Shshsh." Condon put a finger to his lips. There were voices in the public bar.

"Bloody Gyppos . . ." An Anglo-Irish roar. "Regular circus. At least the Yids can fight."

". . . died in the frost," cried a carrying female version of the same. "I've started more under glass."

"Well, here's to old Terry then. Chin-chin and *mort aux vaches*."

"What'd you join, Terry? French Foreign Legion?"

"No, we're . . ."

"Make mine a Bloody Mary."

Condon dug an elbow into Hennessy's side. "Tell me," he whispered in agitation, "why am I whispering? Why do fellows like that roar and you and me lower our voices in public? It's our country, isn't it?"

Hennessy shrugged. "Rowdies," he said contemptuously.

But that wasn't it. Hennessy hadn't lived with the English the way Condon had and couldn't know. It was all arrogance: the roars, the titters. All and always. Condon knew. Wasn't he married to one? Old Hennessy was looking at him oddly. A soapy customer. Don't trust. Think, quickly now, of something soothing. Right. His knight's costume tonight in the bedroom pier-glass. Spurs, epaulets, his own patrician nose: mark of an ancient race. The image, fondly dandled, shivered and broke the way images do. Ho-old it. Patrician all right. A good jaw. Fine feathers—ah no, no. More to it than that. The *spirit* of the Order was imbuing him. Mind over matter. Condon believed in that order of things. Like the Communion wafer keeping fasting saints alive over periods of months. He was a reasoning man—trained in the law—but not narrow, acknowledged super-rational phenomena. More things, Horatio—how did it go? Membership in an ancient religious Order *must* entail an infusion of grace. Tonight was the ceremony to swear in new members. Condon being one. An important, significant moment for him, as he tried to explain to Elsie. But she was spiritually undeveloped.

"A sort of masonry then?" she'd asked when he'd told her how all the really influential Dublin businessmen . . . Certainly NOT or, anyway, not only. Why, the Order dated back nine hundred years. But the English cared only for their own pageantry: Chelsea pensioners, their bull-faced queen. Circuses! Ha! He hated their pomps, had been personally colonized but had thrown off the yoke, his character forming in recoil. Did she *know*, he wondered now as often, how thoroughly he had thrown it off? Did she? He saw himself, two hours ago, coming down the stairs, waiting, one flight up, knee arched, for her admiration. She was in the kitchen.

"Elsie."

"What?"

"Come here."

"Come here yourself. I'm not a dog."

"I want to show you something." That spoiled the surprise but she wouldn't come if he didn't beg. "Please, Elsie." He thought he might be getting pins and needles. Hand on the pommel of his sword, he waited.

"Huwwy then, because the oven . . ." She bustled into the hall, wiping her hands on a cloth. A lively, heavily painted woman in her forties, sagging here and there but still ten times quicker than himself in her movements. "Ho!" she checked and roared. "Tito Gobbi, no less! Or is it Wichard Tucker. You're not going *out* in it?"

Envy!

He walked down the stairs, minding his cloak. "What's for dinner?"

"Steak and kidney pie."

"My ulcer!"

"You haven't a nerve in your body. How could you have an ulcer?"

Her cooking still undermined him—the first thing he had dared notice when he'd attended those parties of hers in Scunthorpe. He'd been a filler-in then: the extra bachelor asked to balance the table. The tight velvet of her evening trousers had drawn his attention and the display of Sheffield plate. It was on his own sideboard now. ("Mr. Condon likes his gwub," she'd noted.) The "w" she put in "Patrick" when she began to use his name impressed him. He thought for a while it might be upper-class. ("I sweat bwicks when Patwick tells a joke!") It was a relief as well as a disappointment when she turned out to be a housekeeper who had married her ageing employer. When the old man died within a year of marriage, Condon rallied round. Mourning enhanced her attractiveness but sat lightly on her. She was quick—giddy, he thought now—and he couldn't keep up with her, seemed to get heavier when he tried. Even her things turned hostile. He remembered the day her electric lawn-mower ran off with him. Weeping with rage, he had struggled to hold it as it plunged down the area slope and crashed through the kitchen window—with himself skidding behind: Handy Andy, Paddy-the-Irishman! The servants were in stitches. He didn't dare ask her not to mention it, could still hear her tell the story—how many times?—to neighbours over summer drinks on the wretched lawn: "And away it wan with pooah Patwick!" They had neighed, hawhawed, choked themselves. He hated them. Buggers to a man. Bloody snobs in their blazers with heraldic thingamybobs on the pockets. Always telling him off. ("In England, people don't say 'bloody'!" " 'Bugger' is rather a strong term over here, old man!" So well it might be!) What he'd put up with! And if you *didn't* put up with it you had no sense of humour. Well, their day was done. India, Ghana, Cyprus, even Rhodesia . . . Little Ireland had shown the way. Let England quake! The West's awake! The West, the East—which of them cared for England now?

"Ah Jesus, that stuff's out of date," Patrick's cousin told him when he came back to live in Ireland. "Our economy is linked to England's. Let the dead bury the dead! And isn't your wife English?"

Her! He looked at her scraping out the remnants of pastry from the dish. Greedy! But she kept her figure. People admired her. "A damn fine woman," they told Patrick who was half pleased and half not. He had never forgiven her evasion of his embrace in the car coming from the church ceremony and the way she had lingered in the hotel bar before making for their bedroom. He had lingered too but, damn it, that was understandable. *He* was chaste, whereas she—decadent product of a decadent country. Bloomy and scented like a hot-house flower warmed by the trade winds of the Empire.

"Why are you looking at me like that?"

"I was thinking", Patrick said, "we Irish are a spiritual people! All that about the Celt having one foot in the grave, you know? Well, the older I get, the truer I know it to be."

She hooted.

"I suppose you don't want pudding?"

"What?"

"Apple charlotte."

He held out his plate. "No cream?"

"Oh Patwick! Your waist bulge!"

"I *want* cream."

He scattered sugar on the brown cliffs of his charlotte. Brown, crumbly hills and crags such as the Knights must have defended against Turks and Saracens. The Irish branch to which Patrick belonged, lacking aristocratic quarterings, had a merely subsidiary connection, but Patrick managed to forget this and anyway *she* would never know. He took and ate the last brown bastion of charlotte from his plate.

She was fidgeting with hers. Afraid of carbohydrates. Her contaminated beauty excited him and sometimes, when she was asleep beside him, he would lean over and, between the ball and finger and thumb, fold the wrinkles into uglier grooves. Smoothing them, he could almost restore her to her peak, a time when men used to look after her and draw, with final cocks of the head in his direction, interrogation marks in the air: how, their wonder grilled him, had *she* come to marry *him*? How? Mmpp! Small mystery there when you came down to brass tacks. Widow's nerves. She wanted a man. Anything— he lambasted himself—in trousers. *Much* more to the point was the question: why had *he* married her? He was a man given to self-query. Pious practices—meditation, examination of conscience—imposed by the various rules he had embraced had revealed to Condon the riches of his own mind. It was theatre to him who had rarely been to a theatre if not to see a panto at Christmas. The first plushy swish of the curtain—he kept his thoughts sealed off in social moments lest one surface and reveal itself—the first dip into that accurately spotlit darkness, when he had a spell of privacy, was as stimulating as sex. How, to-day's Mind demanded of yesterday's, had it made itself up? Why? What if it had it to do over again? Any regrets. Any guidelines for the future? Doppel-ganging Condons stalked his own mental boards. *Why had he married* was a favoured theme to ponder on drives down the arteries of Ireland—frequent since Elsie, despite his work being in Dublin, had insisted on buying a "gentleman's residence" in County Meath. "Why?" he would ask himself, as the tyres slipped and spun through wintery silt or swerved from a panicky rabbit. "Why? Why?— Ah, sure I suppose I was a bit of a fool! Yes." Marriage had looked like a ladder up. It had proved a snake. "A bit of a fool in those days, God help us." Better to marry than to burn—but what if you burned within marriage?

Condon still awoke sweating from nightmare re-enactments of that First Night. "Saint Joseph," he still muttered, as he fought off the dream, "Patron of Happy Families, let me not lose respect for her!" ("Patwick", she used to say, "is a tew-wible old Puwitan! Of course that makes things such fun for him! It's being Iwish!") He had gone to complain and confess to an English priest who reassured him. It was all natural, an image of Divine Love. Condon knew better, but let himself be swayed. Hours after she had said good night he, stiffened by a half-bottle of port from her former husband's stock, would mount the stairs, stumble briefly about in the bathroom and, to a gurgle of receding water, in darkness and with a great devastation of springs, land on the bed of his legal paramour. ("Patwick! You make me feel like Euwo-o-opa!") So let her. Who'd turned whom into an animal? If this is natural, natural let it be! Her cries were smothered, her protests unheeded. The swine revenged themselves on Circe: multiplied, enormous, he snuffled, dug, burrowed, and skewered ("Patwick, you might *shave*!") flattening, tearing, crushing, mauling, then rolling away to the other end of the bed to remark, "I see the hedge needs clipping. Have to see to it. Sloppy!" For his spirit refused to follow where his flesh engaged. He felt embarrassed afterwards, preferred not to breakfast with her and took to slipping out to a hotel where he was able, as a bonus, to eat all he wanted without hearing remarks about calories.

Tonight he would be taking a vow of Conjugal Chastity, promising "to possess his vessel in sanctification and honour". (Ha! Put a stop to *her* gallop!) Formerly, Knights' wives had been required to join in the oath—imagine Elsie: a heretic—but that practice had been abolished. Fully professed Knights took vows of celibacy.

Condon had long concluded that Elsie's appeal for himself had lain in her Protestantism. Bred to think it perilous, he had invested her and it with a risky phosphorescence. Which had waned. Naturally enough. Marooned, the buoyant Medusa clogs to the consistency of gelatine, and what had Prostestantism turned out to be but a set of rules and checks? More etiquette than religion. Elsie got the two mixed up. He doubted that she saw a qualitative difference between adultery and failure to stand up when a woman came into the room.

"A bahbawwian," she'd start in, the minute some poor decent slob like Hennessy was well out the door. "The man's a bahbawwian! You've buwwied me among the beastly Hottentots!"

His people.

"No, Patwick! They are *not* fwiendly! It's all a fwaud! They're cold and sniggewing and smug! Bahbawwians!"

Well, there was no arguing with prejudice. And he knew right well what it was she missed in Ireland: smut and men making passes at her. What she'd have liked would be to hobnob with the Ascendancy. Hadn't she wanted to follow the hunt tomorrow?

"The foliage will be glowious! Amanda's keeping two places in her jeep. I'd have thought you'd have wanted to *see* the countwy. You *talk* enough about Ireland."

He didn't. He hated land untamed by pavements, had a feeling it was cannibalic and out to get him. Explicable: his ancestors had been evicted *off* it after toiling and starving *on* it. He'd got his flinty profile from men pared down by a constant blast of misfortune.

"Please, Patwick. I told the Master we'd follow."

"No."

The word "Master" embarrassed him. He hated hunts: the discomfort of Amanda Shand's jeep rattling his bones over frozen fields and withered heaps of ragweed. Booted and furred, the women would squeal and exchange dirty jokes as they followed the redcoats ("Pink, Patwick! Please!") on their bloody pursuit down lanes like river-beds where brass bedsteads served as slatternly gates, and untrimmed brambles clawed.

"I'm spending the night at the club. I can't make it."

She pouted.

He shrugged.

She made little enough effort with *his* friends, so why should *he* put up with Miss Amanda Shand of Shand House, a trollopy piece, louse-poor but with the Ascendancy style to her still: vowels, pedigree dogs. The dogs she raised for a living, and was reputed to have given up her own bed to an Afghan bitch and litter. But, until the roof fell in on them, those people kept up the pretence. Elsie could have helped consolidate his position—he'd hoped for this—if she'd been the hostess here that she'd been in Scunthorpe. He needed friends. He was a briefless barrister and had been too long abroad. She could have increased his support so easily if she'd turned her charm on his clerical relatives. But no. *They* didn't stand up when she came into a room.

"A priest in this country takes precedence over a woman, Elsie."

"You've buwwied me among the beastly Hottentots!"

And tears. And accusations. Why did he leave her to moulder here? She'd given him the best years of her life. Why shouldn't she come to his meeting tonight? Even Masons had a women's night.

Masons!

"The military monks, to whose Order I have the honour to belong, were celibate. There is no place for women in our ceremonies."

More tears. He stayed on guard. In a long war, victory can be short-lived and tears a feint. When she said:

"Don't you care for me any more?"

He answered, "I love nobody but Jesus."

"Oh!" Her mouth fell open unguardedly and showed her fillings. "Jesus!" she repeated. "Jesus!" She used a little scream and ran out of the room.

In the old days, she used to flatten him with humour. But then, on her own ground, she'd had a gallery. Without one, Jesus became invincible.

Patrick, beginning to feel sorry for her, was pouring her a drink, when the doorbell rang. Hennessy. Patrick put down the glass and ran to head him off. He mustn't come in. A guest would resurrect Elsie who could make him her sounding-board, stooge, straight man and microphone to funnel God knew what bad language and hysteria to the clubs and pubs of half Dublin.

Condon bundled Hennessy down the stairs and back into his car.

"Right you are," Hennessy kept acquiescing. "Right, right, Condon. We'll have a drink in the local. I love pubs. Nice and relaxed. Fine, don't give it a thought."

Voices from the public bar:

"Remember that time the U.N. took a contingent of Paddies to the Congo? No, dear, *not* the Irish Guards, the Free State Army. All dressed in bullswool. *That's* what they call it, cross my heart. No, of course *I* don't know is it from bulls, but it *is* as thick as asbestos and thorny as a fairy rath. And off they went dressed up to their necks in it to the Congo. Left, right, left, right, or whatever *that* is in Erse."

"To the tropics."

"Must have been cooked to an Irish stew."

"Ready for the cannibals."

"Which reminds me, Amanda, where are we dining?"

"Not with me, dears, I haven't a scrap in the place."

So Amanda Shand was there. Patrick drank morosely. Hennessy stood up and said he had to go where no one could go for him. Patrick reflected that Hennessy was a bit vulgar sometimes all right. A bit of a Hottentot.

"... hear the one about the two old Dublin biddies discussing the Congo. One says a neighbour's son has been 'caught by the Balloobas' 'By the Balloobas, dija say, Mrs. ?' says her crony. 'Oh *that* musta been terrible painful!' "

Laughter.

"And the one about . . ."

Patrick closed his ears. Hear no, see no, think no evil. Difficult. It wormed its way everywhere, sapped the most doughty resistances.

He thought of a visit he had made that morning to a clerical cousin confined in a home for mad priests—a disagreeable duty but Patrick had felt obliged. Blood was thicker than water and he had promised his aunt he'd go. He'd come away feeling tainted. Weakness flowed like a contagion from Father Fahy. A mild fellow, shut up because of his embarrassing delusions, he thought himself the father of twelve children with a wife expecting a thirteenth.

"I don't mind the number," he had confided to Condon, "I'm not superstitious about such matters. As a priest . . ." The smile flicked off and on. It was not impressive, for his teeth fitted badly and there were no funds to get inmates new ones. As long as he stayed shut up here, ecclesiastical authority saw little point in throwing good money after bad. "Poor Anna is worn out, tense, you know, frayed. She worries about our eldest, Brendan, who's up in the College of Surgeons and . . ." The priest had names and occupations for every member of his imagined brood. "You know yourself, Patrick, women . . ."

Fahy confided doubts about the Holy Father's policy with regard to birth-control. "Poor Anna is a literal believer," he groaned, "a simple woman." He must have been a bad priest, a shirker. Wasn't he trying to shift anxieties, which had sifted through the confessional grating, on to Patrick himself, the confessor's confessor? Distasteful that a priest should imagine a wife for himself with such domestic clarity! How far, one tried to wonder, *did* the imaginings go? Bad times. Our Blessed Lady had foretold as much in 1917 to the children at Fatima. "My Son", she had said, "has drawn back His hand to smite the world. I am holding it back but my arm grows tired." It must be numb by now. Well, Patrick was doing his bit, joining the Knights: a warrior against the forces of darkness. War. The language of the Church was heady with it but practice dampeningly meek. St. George had been struck off the register of saints.

"No, no and no, I won't be beaten down!" Amanda Shand's voice rose in a flirtatious shriek. "The doggies are my bread and butter! Damn it all, Terry, I'm a single girl and . . ."

Girl, thought Condon. Forty if she was a day. Selling one of her hounds. That sort lived by myth: distressed lady, *morya*. Couldn't take a *real* job because if she worked from nine to five as a secretary, she would *be* a secretary. Dabbling in dog-breeding she could live off the smell of an oil rag and be a lady still. He doubted she saw meat more than once a week. Patrick had no patience with the like. Where was Hennessy? Bit of prostatic trouble there. What were we but future worm-food?

"Seriously . . ." Terry's voice now. "It's the youth. I hope I'm no old fogy. I'm thirty-nine and like my bit of fun. I don't mind long hair or free love or any of that, but I think they've lost sight of some jolly important matters, what with all this fraternizing with nigs and . . ."

"*Who's* going out to fight for nig-nogs, Terry? Bet you don't even know which side you'll be on!"

"Right! You're absolutely right. I don't give a damn which side I'm on. They're all black to me, haha. No, but I do have a purpose. I think the next great war will be with the coloureds. Don't laugh! I mean *they'll* be attacking us. Look at South Africa, Rhodesia, the U.S. They've got the message. It's easy for us to sit on our bums in Southern Ireland—the last country where a gentleman is recognized as such, by the way, which is why I like it here—to sit here on our bums and disapprove of the white supremacists. Much too easy. It may be less so in the future. Look at China. Count them up. They want what we've got, right? Right. I don't say I blame the poor buggers but every man's got to fight his own corner. And there isn't enough to go round, right? Besides, a lot of decent things would go down the drain if the West went under. . . . Well, the long and the short of it is I'm going out to fight *for* the nigs in order to train myself to fight *against* them."

"And for the lolly."

"And for the lolly."

"Upon this battle depends the survival of Christian civ., what?"

"Right."

". . . all that we have known and cared for will sink . . ."

Someone, not Terry, began to deliver in tones wavering between drunken parody and drunken sentiment, a speech which slipped through Condon's defences. With astonishment, he realized that he and the rowdies in the bar had something in common. There was that fellow, in his literal, simple way, heeding the call of the times and assuming the military part of the knightly mission at the very moment when Condon himself was shouldering its spiritual side. They complemented each other. Well and why not? Hadn't Protestant volunteers fought the Turk with Catholic knights at the siege of Malta? Patrick stood up. He was thinking of going into the bar when he heard Amanda say:

"Hey, what about giving Elsie a tinkle?"

"Elsie who?"

"Elsie Condom or Condon or whatever. She's got a soft spot for old Terry here and she's sure to produce sandwiches. Her lord and master's almost certain to be off the premises. Bet she'd like to light your fire, Terry, on your last night."

"Got her number?"

"In the book. Listen, it'd be doing a good deed in a naughty world to poke old Elsie. Seriously. She doesn't get much and . . ."

"What about yourself, Amanda . . ."

"Oh *well*, if . . ."

Patrick collided with Hennessy who was finally returning and pushed him, for the second time that evening, backwards out the door and into his own car. A yellow Austin Healey with a GB on its rump was drawn up beside it. Patrick resisted an impulse to give it a passing kick. His mind jumbled thoughts, like a washing-machine throwing about soiled linen and, above it, he managed to chat about how time-was-getting-on-sorry-Hennessy-but-better-be-hitting-the-road-slippery-as-well-be-off-betimes. The man must think he was mad.

Patrick felt a thrust of humiliation knife him. He felt almost tearful. An unskinned part of himself had been reached. He had thought he and Elsie had something, a . . . union . . . a solidarity which . . . In his own head he groped sadly, reaching an unexplored place. Hennessy's voice came to him but he couldn't distinguish the words. He felt exposed, mutilated. Hennessy's Volkswagen funnelled down the hedgy roads. Briars scraped the windows and squeaked.

"There should be a quorum," Hennessy was saying. "We should hold out for that."

"Yes," managed Condon.

"And what's your position on the other matter?"

What matter? Which? Had Hennessy *heard*?

"I . . . what?"

"Are you feeling all right?"

"No. I had a dizzy spell. I'm afraid I missed . . ."

"Oh well, it doesn't matter." Hennessy sounded miffed.

But Condon had to know. "No, no *tell* me."

"I've *been* telling you! Corcoran wants selection of the ambulance corps to be left up to him and his henchmen. A matter of getting the strings into his own hands and . . ."

"Ah."

Condon's mind drifted again. Didn't she *care* for him at all then, if she . . . Oh, and that was what *she* had asked him! He groaned.

"Are you in pain?"

"No, no, slight twinge. My ulcer. . . . Nothing serious."

He *must*, would, pull himself together. Mind over matter. Yes.

The Knights' ceremony was being held in a Dublin hotel. An entire floor had been taken over, but members spilled into corridors and stairs and lobby where, cloaked and armed, they drew the eye, impressing the serf-grey citizenry with their spiritual and temporal pelf. A drunken poet got into the lift with Condon and Hennessy. Pink and pendulous, his nose (Condon reproved himself for thinking) resembled a skinned male organ. The poet fixed the Knights with his tight, urine-yellow goat's eyes and grinned. A notorious lecher, he was not the sort of man with whom either would choose to associate, but they were, as always in Dublin, on nodding terms with him.

"How are things, Ian?"

"A wet old night."

"Ha," roared the poet in a peasant brogue, assumed, as all Dubliners know, to make them feel effete, urban and far from the loamy roots of things. "How are our Knights T-T-Templarss? Still as r-r-rand-d-dy and roistering as when they were burnt at the stake by Philipe le Bel? Burnt," he hissed, "b-b-burrrrntt and their goods confiscated, ha! Not that *that*'s likely to happen again. There's a rising tide of p-p-permiss-ssiveness, as they call it now. Still secret, still underground but about to oo-ooz-z-z-ze up and submerge us all in a f-f-f-foam of s-s-sperm! The age of Eros is upon us. I've just c-come back from the cu-cu-cunty counthrrry where they've been enjoying a spell of warm weather, and yez'd never credit the goings on I witnessed under hedges and d-d-ditches."

"I'm sure we wouldn't," Hennessy told him. "This is our floor." He stepped out with a gelid nod. "Be seeing you." But the poet followed them.

"Maids and matrons," he roared. "Wedded wives f-f-fu-fuck-ck-cking in the f-f-fields. Cuckoo eggs in every nest. Maybe your own spouses are . . ."

Condon hit him. Before he knew it his fist had shot out and caught the pink, wettish—he felt it wet on his knuckles—nose. Or was the wetness blood? It was. His knuckles were stained with it. The poet had been put on a couch and his collar loosened.

"He's O.K. Just a nose-bleed."

"Head back, Ian, hold your head back."

"No, better not. The blood makes you sick. Indigestible. Spit it out. Get us a glass. Thanks. Mind the carpet now."

"Hold his nose over the glass. In, man, in. Poke it in."

"Get him to a bathroom."

"Good thing it happened on this floor. No scandal. How did he get in?"

"Gate-crasher."

A Knight walked up to Condon. "Come and wash your hands too. He's all right, drunk, deserved what he got. Do him a world of good."

Other voices joined in.

"What was it he said about . . . Condon's wife?"

"Shush!" And loudly: "Someone should have done it long ago. A foul-mouthed fellow, a gurrier."

"A fine lesson for him. A low type. You're a hard man, Condon. A true Knight, haha!"

Surrounded by his fellows, Condon felt his agitation abate into a lapping tide of excitement. Someone must have given him a brandy because, as the ceremony began, a manservant in cotton gloves, tapped him on the arm to recover the empty glass. He gave it to the man and himself to rituals he had been studying for some weeks. This was to be a brief and worldly affair because of the hour and place. Mass would be celebrated in the Order's chapel next morning. Would he stay? He had intended to but now was not so sure. The panoply of the differing ranks of Knights and monks confused him. All wore crosses recalling the crusades on which knights had gone leaving wives locked in chastity belts. Or was that myth? Had the first Knights been celibate? And had such contraptions been widely used? Very unsanitary, if so. He had seen one once in a museum. Was it the Cluny museum in Paris? He wasn't sure, reproached himself for not achieving a prayerful mood. *Oh my God, I am heartily sorry for having offended thee, and I detest my sins above every other evil* . . . Did he? He did not! He was glad he had pucked that obscene fellow on the gob. Watch what's happening. You'll miss your cue. The oath of conjugal chastity brought back figures crouching in a corner of his brain: Terry-the-nig-killer and Elsie. Niggers for that sort began at Liverpool. No holds barred with wives of nigs or Papists. No holds barred with any wives in profligate England. Adultery winked at. Since Henry the Eighth. Ruin seize thee, ruthless king, Confusion on they banners wait . . . That was some other . . . *Would* she? NO. Ah no, she was forty-four—still dirty-minded, though, had violated his privacy in talk with Amanda Shand. Don't trust, you can't trust her. Ah God, his knightly honour was a joke, besmirched in advance. Maybe, at this very . . .

He made to leap up but a hand pulled him back, recalling him to the time and place. "Not yet," whispered Hennessy, thinking Condon had mistaken the cues printed on the slips of paper which had been handed out. "Not till after the hymn."

Nigs. Knicks. Patrick sank back on his knees. To think she should spoil a moment of such spiritual significance, dragging his soul down to the level of her own. A stain on one Knight's honour must affect the Order as a whole. Every man responsible for his woman. He had read in the *National Geographic* about adulteresses somewhere in Africa being impaled per vaginam. Punished whereby they had—but the idea was repugnant. Better punish the lover like in *The Cask of Amontillado*. Brick him up. By God if he came home this night and found them at it! Jesus, let them not, because if they . . . Please, Jesus. He'd have no choice. But. Universally recognized. *Crime passionnel.* Juries let off the husband. And the heavenly jury? *Veni creator spiritus* . . . The hymn ended and the Knights rose creakily. Not one was under fifty. Patrick's head reeled and and whirled. Pounded.

"Well now, let's toast our new Knight of Honour and Devotion." Hennessy led him off.

There was no slipping away. They drank fast and garrulously. At one point Condon was sick. He threw up with decorum, in the lavatory, unknown to any. He ate a peppermint to sweeten his breath. Coming back, he brought the conversation round to Parnell and Kitty O'Shea.

"The woman was an adulteress."

"But was it fair to punish her lover and the millions who depended on him? The course of Irish history might . . ."

"You're forgetting the scandal! The scandal to the souls of those same millions! How could the Church . . ."

Rounds of drinks waited, marshalled like skittles. Four brandies had been bought for Patrick. The bar was closing but every man wanted to stand his round. Honour obliged.

Suddenly, Condon said he needed to get home. Urgently. His wife was unwell, subject to giddy spells, and might not hear the phone.

"Can I borrow your car?" he asked Hennessy. "I'll get it back to you tomorrow."

Hennessy gave him the keys.

Patrick took them and rushed out of the hotel, started the car without warming the engine and raced hell-for-leather out of Dublin and into the hedgy embrace of country roads. Here he was forced by an attack of nausea to pull in and found himself, out of the car, weeping in a ditch and embracing a thorn tree. "Elsie," he groaned, to his own astonishment, "Elsie!" He began to roar and bellow like a bull, filling and emptying his lungs with desolate twanging air. After some minutes he got back into the car, feeling wet and so paralytic with cold he could hardly touch his fingers around the stick-shift. He put on the heater and drove in shivering sobriety back across the mountains, concentrating on the road and reciting prayers to calm his nerves. ". . . disease of desire," he whispered mechanically, "to possess his vessel in sanctification and honour, not in the disease of desire as do the Gentiles who know not God . . ."

As he turned into his own winding drive, darkly flanked by rhododendrons, he got a glimpse of Elsie's lighted window and her silhouette, heavier than he had remembered it, closing the curtains. He rounded the last curve and came on the battered yellow Austin Healey which had been parked earlier in the public-house yard. Standing by its nose—he must have been looking at the motor, for the bonnet was raised—like a moth in the glare of Patrick's headlights, was a man in a check sports coat: Terry. Patrick drove straight for him, as though following a traffic signal in the man's gullet. He could see into the pulsing throat and even the flap on the uvula glistening against the dark interior. There was a thump. Patrick's head hit the headrest behind him. The man fell forward on to the Volkswagen then, on the rebound, into the unbonneted engine of his own car. Heels up, arms flopping, he was carried backwards as the two cars pursued their course into a tree. The Austin Healey buckled, the man's limbs crunched within the integument of his clothes. Patrick—although he was to prove to be suffering from minor concussion—felt nothing.

Moments later, Elsie found his cloaked figure, bending over the wreckage, howling in the elated, almost musical accents of dogs on a moonlit night. "I *did* it. Jesus, I did it."

That version never got out.

Connections rallied. Witnesses testified that the Englishman had been drinking heavily in the pub. They surmised he must have lost his way and strayed up Condon's driveway in search of the cross-roads. In all likelihood, he would have neglected to turn on his lights. That Condon should round the bend of his own driveway at an incautious speed was understandable at so late an hour in a gentleman tired after a long drive and eager to get home to his bed. A regrettable accident.

Terry's friends waked him jovially, pleased with the excuse for a little extra drinking. "After all", said Amanda Shand, "he was only a bird of passage." The Condons, she has heard, were getting on together as never before. He had taken her for a change of scene to Malta and *she* had sent Amanda a card saying she was "having a whale of a time".

A Travelled Man

Mrs. Thorne met Vanni at the opera. It was the Maggio Musicale in Florence and a client had given him a ticket which he had, regretfully, been unable to sell. He kissed Mrs. Thorne's hand, smiled and mimed his good will.

"Wags his tail a lot, doesn't he?" was her comment to her husband.

The curtain-raiser had been *La Serva Padrona*, an opera in which Vespone, a valet, manages to promote true love and defeat the pomps of the Establishment without singing a note —the part, of course, being taken by a mime. Mrs. Thorne referred to Vanni afterwards as "Vespone".

"Isn't our Vespone a rather obsolete type in today's Italy?"

"He's a victim of Vatican roulette," Mr. Thorne told her. "His wife keeps having babies. I gather he hopes to become a state archivist but can't work for the qualifying exam. He does research for foreign scholars—he's done some for me—so as to make a little cash and this takes all his time. The exam has an English-language requirement and he can hardly pass *that* by mime."

"Poor Vespone."

"Yeah, I guess he really is an obsolete figure: Lucca's last scribe. He lives in Lucca. He can read medieval documents like nobody else. Half the theses submitted in the field in the last ten years are based on his research. Unacknowledged. He's the native guide to an occupying army of scholars."

Vanni looked the part: an ageing urchin with a twitch to his eye. His ridiculously old clothes recalled neo-realist films and, even after the Boom, when every solvent Italian had graduated from scooter to car, he was still to be seen on a bike. It was an aged, angular object which reminded people unpleasantly of thin times and Italy's humiliation after the war. So did Vanni himself. Contemporaries avoided him. Passers-by were moved by outmoded impulses: men groped through trouser-pockets for a touch at their privates to ward off *iettatura* from that twitchy eye; women let fingers rest inside handbags on the talismanic metal of their Yale keys.

"I don't see why you don't try for that exam again," goaded Anna, his wife. "Make some use of those Americans who exploit you. Get practice. Speak English to them!"

But when he tried, Vanni's mind spun like a pinball machine amuck. Words evaded him. His appalled eyeballs rolled and he began to shake. This could happen even when he wasn't speaking English for he drank too much bitter black coffee, got too little sleep.

"My wife thinks I am a fool," he told the archivists, and his lids blinked. "She says everyone makes use of me and underpays me." Guying himself, he shrugged and trembled humorously inside a suit which bore traces of carefully cleaned oil stains down the front.

"My American friends are fond of me," he said hopefully.

"Of what they can get out of you," said his wife.

"No," said Vanni, "of me."

"Poor sucker," said his wife.

"*Sul serio.*"

"*Fesso!*"

So he felt greatly vindicated when Mrs. Thorne offered him a six-month appointment at Laurelgrove College, Los Angeles, at a salary which tripled what he could normally hope to make in a year, plus expenses. It was a private college (endowed by Mrs. Thorne's father) where he was to teach paleography so as to wipe the eye of rival institutions which had not thought of offering such a course. Mrs. Thorne would help him with English and he would give her Italian lessons.

"You can stay with us," she said. "We have a Hollywood mansion too big for the pair of us. We rattle around in it."

Vanni did not take this seriously. People he knew stayed only with relatives and then only if their house burned down or they were far from home on military service. Besides, he had no dressing-gown. Still, he mentioned the offer to his wife.

"Does she mean it?"

"About staying with them? Just polite talk, wouldn't you think?"

"What's the husband?"

"I've told you. A client. An art historian. They turned up last May while you were at your mother's and took me to dinner at Otello's. We had white truffles," he recalled. "When I said I wanted to learn English, she made this offer. Now she's written to confirm it."

"You could save", his wife reflected, "all you earn if you stayed with them. Enough to make a down payment on a house. Then we could get out of here. Take her up on that offer. Keep them sweet. Butter them up. A soft tongue costs nothing. And while you're there remember to keep out of bars . . . (et cetera)."

"All right." Vanni agreed.

Anna mended and packed his clothes, encouraged him to have a suit made on tick and gave a dinner-party for him before he left. She invited their closest relatives and spent days preparing a complicated menu and dragging furniture from their poky dining-room into the yard. She even got hold of a sweet-smelling brazier to cover the smell from their neighbour's septic tank. She'd been to the hairdresser, he noticed. Poor thing, she could rarely afford it. Tired, she let him fill her glass too often during dinner and, when he put his arms around her afterwards in bed, wept and confessed jealousy at his leaving for the rich freedom of America.

"I'm thirty-five," she sobbed. "It's an awful age."

"I'll bring you back some miracle creams."

"I haven't always been nice."

"Neither have I."

"Write."

"Yes."

"*Real* letters. And, Vanni, save all you can. Sponge! Don't try to cut a fine figure there. Remember your life is here. Bring back all you can."

Fetched our guest from the airport.

Jim much the same: fixes drinks and takes out the garbage; otherwise just *sits* or sits and turns the pages of an art book. Blames me. Denies he does. Refuses to see an analyst.

I'm going to give a party for his fiftieth birthday. Rub his nose in it! Paunchy bastard! It will be a chance to introduce Vanni to some people. I'll let Jim think that's *all* it's for, then surprise him with a cake. Fifty fat phallic candles burning soft grease into the sugar!

Los Angeles

My dear Anna,

I did not write again until after my first classes so as to be able to tell you how they went. Really, quite well. Mrs. Thorne had coached me. I got my first cheque this morning and enclose it. I think that as long as I can manage to stay with the Thornes I shall need very little for myself. . . .

I gave the party. The usual farts came, pinched each other's wives' arses and left the place stinking like a tavern. I'd sent Jim out about eight to look for ice, telling him I'd invited a couple of people in to meet Vanni. When he got back the drive was full of cars, but he'd been seen and had to come in. The gang was primed to sing *Happy Birthday to Youoooo* the moment he opened the door. I knew he'd hate that. Then I tripped forward with the cake: a frilly memorial to the fifty winters that besiege his cock. He carried the thing off well enough.

My dear Anna,

. . . a party. People were kind but I was glad I couldn't speak English: it was an excuse. I am no good in social gatherings . . . dreadful food . . . a lot of talk about politics. Mrs.

Thorne is concerned with some organization on race relations, I think, but she has so many interests that I get confused. She has two poodle puppies which someone gave her. The black one is called Black Power and the brown one Brown (Latin-American) Power. Of course they are really called Blackie and Brownie. They kept piddling all over the carpet and people followed them about with bottles of Vichy water which, it seems, contains an antidote to the acid in their pee.

Jim has developed a boil on his ass. I have not been invited to inspect it. Very private all of a sudden about his person, he has removed himself from our bedroom and sleeps permanently now on the divan in his study. I suppose it is a psychosomatic boil. Vanni seems hopelessly shy.

Imagine, Anna, an immense garden suburb where nobody ever walks. I must ask my hostess for a lift even to post this letter. People are isolated here, stuck together like belly and shirt.

Alice Thorne rejected the courtesies whereby Vanni had hoped to contribute towards his keep. She did not want doors opened, parcels carried or errands run. She did not even like him to stand when she came into a room. Vanni, unable to remember this, kept bouncing upwards like a slapped ball.

"For God's sake, Vanni, we want you to feel this is your home. *Relax!*"

But he *had* dissatisfied her. He would not drink her cocktails which upset his liver and he evaded questions about his personal life.

"I like to know people are getting a kick out of life. You should be having yourself a ball while you're here, Vanni. It's your first trip out of Italy and you're not enjoying it to the full! Say: you know the root of the trouble? It's that you don't drive. Now here's my suggestion. Take our third car and get some driving lessons in it. I'll drop you off at the school. You can arrange to have a lesson during my gym class."

"Thank you, Mrs. Thorne, but: no. Really, I prefer not."

"Now why be so negative, Vanni? It would be good for you to learn to drive. Give you confidence in yourself. Don't you know that to be without a car in L.A. is like being without legs any place else? Now, just you tell me where you've been and what you've seen since you arrived? Have you visited the Music Center? No. Marine Land? No. Have you see Watts?"

She catechized him severely. "*I* haven't time or I'd drive you round the points of interest myself."

"Oh no, no, thank you, Mrs. Thorne."

"Alice."

"Eh?"

"Alice. Call me Alice."

"Yes: Alice. I mean: no. I don't want you to give up your time to me."

"Then take driving lessons."

He resisted. His reason shamed him and did not occur to her: the cost. Later, it struck him that perhaps he was around the house too much and getting on her nerves. He took to spending days in the college library, lunching and sometimes dining out of the food-machines in the men's locker-room.

"I goofed," said Mrs. Thorne to Vanni whom she had picked up at the college after his class. "I can't drive you to the house right away. Jim made an appointment for me with my masseur. Hostility: it's his way of making me feel a fat slob. Which it has. I'm skipping lunch. Why don't you lunch at Dino's? I'll pick you up there after my session. I'll bet you're crazy to eat some spaghetti! Don't overdo it now or you'll be having to join us in the gym!" She wagged her finger at him as he stepped out of the car and into the clutches of the buttons.

Since there was no avoiding an expensive lunch, Vanni ordered a half-bottle of Chianti *classico*. His body had been maladjusted for weeks, craving familiar flavours.

"Chianti doesn't travel," he was told. "Have some Valpolicella or a nice Californian wine. Try an Inglenook. Are you a tourist?"

Vanni told the man—an Italian? An Italo-American?—that he was working in the local college.

"A professor," said the fat man. "My son's at law school. Anyone can go to school here. You got the dough, you can go to school."

"In Italy too," Vanni remarked.

"Yeah?" The man considered. "That's true." He decided to be an Italian. "We had schools back there when they were running round here shooting each other like savages. They had no *time* for schooling then," he reflected doubtfully. "No, sir! Tell you what you'd better watch out for here," he slid on to a more congenial topic. "Women."

"Women?"

"They're dynamite. Especially the older ones. Round heels. They're hot for Italian men too." The fat man winked, his loyalties reconciled. "They love us," he said. "Yeah, you bet. They're like female hamsters. Did you ever watch a female hamster? No? Well, my son has them. Not the one that's doing law. His kid brother. He's nine and I said to my wife, 'Ssabout time that kid learned some biology.' So I got him these hamsters. Educational, get it? They're funny little things: soft, cappuccino-coloured and no bigger than a child's fist, but, brother, you should see that female when she wants her male! And when she doesn't—do you know what she does? She eats his balls off."

"His . . . ?"

"Yeah," said the fat man. "*Le palle. I coglioni.* You'd better believe me."

"Enjoy your lunch?" asked Alice Thorne.

"Thank you very much," said Vanni.

"You mean: 'very much, thank you'!"

"Do I?"

"Uhuh. Bet you overate. Let's feel the paunch." She slipped a lean hand inside his lower waistcoat. Vanni slid sideways from her along the car seat. She followed. "Aha!" With relish. "Guilty! Fat," she shouted. "Why are you squirming?"

"I'm ticklish."

"Goodness!" She pinched him. "How heavily armoured you are! All those buttons!" Eyes with whiskey-coloured whites looked into his. She had a hamsterish complexion too—muddy. Her nose twitched. Vanni caught her marauding hand and returned it to the steering wheel.

"My, Vanni, you have problems!"

"Problems, Mrs. Thorne?"

"Come off it. Stop rejecting me." Her thick-capped teeth were merrily bared. Her finger-nails too were larger than life due, she had explained, to the gelatine she dissolved every morning in her orange juice. "Makes them tough as horses' hooves!" But they were more like claws: yellowish and coarse with a slight curve to the tip. "I guess you know me well enough by now to call me 'Alice'?" she asked ironically. "And for me to ask why you get uptight when a woman gets near you? Jim's worried. He asked me did I think you were a fairy? You know: *finocchio*. I looked it up."

"Oh."

"You've got a reputation to live up to—a European scholar and all! Our little Sophomores were expecting an Abelard."

Vanni placed his brief-case protectively on his lap.

"Nobody's like that now," he told her. "We work. We . . . sublimate." He produced the word with pride: a linguistic fence taken.

"Why, Vanni!" Mrs. Thorne swung the car round a corner and towards a kerb. She parked under a carob tree. Under its tent, the green-tinted windows sealed them off as intimately as a pastoral bower. "Vanni," she faced him, "don't you *know* that a truly adult sexual drive cannot be sublimated? That according to modern analytic theory . . ."

She lost him.

"Emotional maturity", she pressed, "is . . ."

What did she want? Was she a trifle unbalanced? The Change? Vanni's mind slid from such dank unsoundnesses. Should he move out of her house? What an expense though!

How explain it to Anna? The truth—supposing that what he had begun to suspect *was* the truth—would arouse her sturdy derision. *"You,"* he quailed at her imagined cackle, "why should she pick on *you*? She'd have to be hard up. Unless you led her on? No, you just wanted to stay in one of those motels and . . ." And what? Fritter his substance? Chase Hollywood starlets? Spend money in bars? Vanni, recoiling from Anna's rebukes, found himself listening again to Mrs. Thorne. She was complaining about Jim. The husband. Wanted to confide. Well, that was all right. *Wasn't* it? His was a captive ear and it was as well to know what service was required.

"I'm boring you?"

"No, no," he protested. "Not at all. I would so much like to help."

"Vanni," she seized his surrendered hand in both of hers.

He quashed the feeling that she had a third hand poised to clutch some other part of him.

"Vanni, you're a beautiful human being!"

Seconds passed. Vanni's imprisoned hand twitched. Held too long, their iconic pose grew embarrassing. *She* seemed unable to extricate herself. *He* was resolved to make no move.

"Well," the hands unclenched, "better fish or cut bait!" A hand landed lightly on his fly. She grimaced. "Not rising? Ah well, ya can't win 'em all!" Grinning, she turned on the motor and swung the car back to the boulevard.

Cocktail time.

"Hi, Vanni," Mrs. Thorne raised a highball. "Jim and I have been discussing LOVE the old perennial. He thinks young people are more idealistic than our generation was. What do you say?"

"In Italy", Vanni fished for a cautious cliché, "we perhaps distinguish more between love and sex."

Thorne nodded vigorously.

His wife looked sour. "And between both and economics?" she asked.

"Alice!" Thorne sighed.

"Or are these things frankly formulated in your culture, Vanni?"

"Love . . ." began Vanni warily, uncertain what he had said wrong.

"Oh, what's *that*?" Mrs. Thorne hammered the word angrily. "What's *love*?"

Her Hallowe'en grin contrasted with the fierce crackle of her voice. "Well, what is it? Having hot pants for someone? The search for an empteenth maternal bag of waters to cleanse oneself in? An unguent of youth to rub on the ageing member? It used", she was bridling her voice so tightly now, each breath was a small explosion, "to be held that an old man, if he slept with a young girl, could draw her youth from her. Like cannibals eating the hearts of those whose qualities they envy! Ha!" She laughed noisily, ending in a faint scream. "Haghaagh!"

Thorne left the room.

Vanni buried his nose in his Campari glass.

"Sorry," said his hostess. "Nothing to do with you."

She went into the kitchen whence presently a din reminded him of Anna who also cooked when exasperated. He remembered a maenad whirling wet lettuce, splashing vinegar into oil, driving moon-shaped meat choppers across ragged cutting-boards to reduce some herbal mixture and, in her mind, for all he knew, some vulnerable part of himself to aromatic pulp.

"I made fifty dollars today," Mrs. Thorne told Vanni.

They were having a conversation lesson, speaking into a tape recorder which Vanni could subsequently replay in order to check the inadequacies of his English accent.

"How did you make them?" he asked.

"I sold some LSD I'd got from some chemistry students. I'd intended taking it myself, then I lost my nerve. It seemed silly to waste it, so I told my dentist he could have it for fifty dollars. He accepted. I guess that makes me a pusher."

"What is a pusher, please?"

"Someone who sells drugs. It's against the law, so don't mention it to anyone. Considering the way Jim just scatters money as though it fell from heaven, I feel perfectly justified in picking up what I can where I can."

"Yes."

"This is supposed to be a conversation lesson, Vanni. *Say something.*"

"I think perhaps I have not much to say."

"You can say that again."

"Please?"

"Forget it. Look: teach me some more proverbs. How do you say 'Sticks and stones can break my bones but names will never hurt me'? In Italian."

"Repeat again, please."

She did.

"Ah, *'la lingua non ha osso, ma rompe il dosso'*. I translate: 'The tongue has no bones but can break your back.' It is the opposite I think."

"I guess", said Mrs. Thorne, "it depends on what society you live in."

Vanni discovered a bus. The only other passengers were three black women wearing pastel nylon livery and an old man asleep on the back seat. Still it was a bus and its rhythms were pleasantly familiar to Vanni who had been a passenger on public transport all his life. They helped reassure him that he was he and here was real: propositions constantly combated in his mind since his arrival. He was addled by misgivings about the value of services rendered, benefits received and whether he was earning his keep. Did the Thornes want him out? Or was their polite pressure to stay to be accepted at face value? He couldn't decide. Every night his doubts were translated into dreams in which he was back in Italy having missed his plane, was here but had lost his pay-cheque, was being held up to public shame for trying to seduce Alice Thorne or to private ridicule for failing to do so. Daily, he awoke with a dolphin's leap, a sense of inadequacy, a compulsion to rush to an airport, bank or post office. He would have his pants half on and his feet in his socks before realizing that it was only 5 a.m. Back in sleep, fresh fears menaced until eight when he got up and accepted the day. But his acceptance was never total. He watched the Thornes' behaviour for the oblique signals whereby real as opposed to official meanings are conveyed. The apparent absence of this secondary channel confused and kept him on edge. It was possible that Americans might mean no more than they said but more probable that he was failing to pick up messages. A dimension was lacking to his life and, worse, to his relations with his hosts. He went about in a prickle of guilt.

Today, however, he was off duty. Alone.

The frontboard of the bus promised "Ocean" and that ocean was the Pacific. "*Il Pacifico,*" Vanni whispered. The word burrowed to a layer of old memory: schooldays and adventure stories. *Magellano, Balbao, il Pacifico.* Nacreous syllables, preserved in the deep-freeze of oblivion, thawed now with a double radiance, at once youthful and nostalgic. He had scarcely remembered them since. Travel posters did not address themselves to the like of Vanni Moncini. Or so he had supposed. Whereas! Ha! *Conquistador!* He derided and warmed to a wave of boyish pleasure.

But the ocean was miles off yet. They headed west. The tracts of urbs traversed grew more and more sub. Ephemeral structures sold instant snacks: tacos, tamales, burgers, root beer, Colonel Sanders' Southern-Fried Chicken-in-a-bucket. Vanni watched velvety lawns give way to balding ones. Familiar latitudes. He enjoyed the passage through streets full of lower-middle-class houses, chewed up gardens, toys, bicycles. Dust hung on banana fronds. As he stepped down at the terminus, he saw graffiti carved deep in the flesh of a cactus, sniffed unhygienic smells with exhilaration.

"What's this place?" he asked the bus driver.

"Venice. Straight ahead for the ocean."

Vanni set out. He passed the "Bible Mission": a clapboard giant's shoe-box whose sign winked "Jesus Saves" at him in red neon. Plastic flags fluttered in a dealer's yard. In tinsel sleighs, early Santa Clauses rode above the boulevard, their glitter lost in the sunlight. An Esso sign. More clapboard. The known and the unknown, the cosy and the unforeseen. Vanni longed for an encounter. He progressed past façades as wilfully quaint as those at Viareggio and—was at the sea. A grey marbled expanse: only its edges curled as each slow oily wave unfurled itself. Vanni, feeling as incautious as Ulysses—blamed by Dante for travelling off the known map—shed a shoe and stuck one yellowish, knobbly, scholar's foot into the water. The caresses were cool as sherbet. Next to him a seabird with tweezer bill probed the sand for worms. "The Other Ocean!" Vanni saluted it and, forgetting what he had been told about water pollution, scooped a palmful to his lips.

A girl stood in front of him: perhaps sixteen years old in a cape of straight metallic hair which touched the tops of her bare thighs.

"Would you like a flower?"

It was a nasturtium.

Vanni took the fiery, sticky-stemmed blossom and tried to put it in his lapel. But the buttonhole had been sewn up behind. He fumbled. "I need a pin."

"Here." She unfastened a white plastic button from somewhere beneath her hair and handed it to him.

He attached the flower and looked at the girl. She paused a few seconds more then, affected perhaps by Vanni's own shyness, swerved and, with a flip of her fingers, ran off across the sand.

He turned back the way he had come. Froth sucked at his ankles. He touched the petals. Should he have suggested something, he wondered? Tea? A trip to a café perhaps? He could at least have asked her what the button meant, strike up a conversation. A girl like that! No guile! He turned to look after her but the sun had slipped down and its afterglow on the wet sand blurred his vision. The girl's sunburnt skin and hair had been much the same colour as the beach. She was camouflaged.

He would have to wait half an hour for a bus. Good. Returning to the Thorne household felt like the return to barracks after a furlough. The Thornes were constantly bickering now and drawing him into their bouts. Eager to please, he sat between them, bobbing, disclaiming, never sure who had been the target of some stealthy spar. It was a strain. Undignified too.

He bought some paper in a drugstore and, over a slice of berry pie—good—and a cup of coffee—tasteless—began a letter to Anna. Pointless to mention his troubles. She would be scathing. Her temper was worn sharp as an old coin by making do. The hollow runnels under her still fine eyes looked, too, like the tracks of lost coins. "My dear Anna. . . ." Frail contact! This bit of flimsy, striated paper would reach her in an unforeseeable mood and when his own had changed. Eight hours difference. Dark night now in Lucca. The watchman sticks coloured slips of paper in the jambs of doors to prove he has made his round. Anna sleeps, her mouth damp on the pillow. What would she like to hear? That I am making money. The U.S. stamp tells her that. "I am lonely," he wrote and enjoyed a gobbet of boysenberry pie. "I get depressed," he added. "I miss you. I am too old to travel alone but I *am* learning the language. . . ." His tongue, as he licked the envelope, was sweet with the taste of Oregon boysenberries. He tossed the letter into a red and blue mail-box.

Vanni had learned to ignore the telephone in his room. It was an extension and never rang for more than two or three peals. By then, the incoming call—never for Vanni—would have been answered by someone elsewhere in the house. Today, however, the instrument, as though briefly inhabited by a poltergeist, kept giving off little quavers, feverish semi-peals and clicks. When he finally picked it up, the receiver bounced in his hand. A young girl's voice was shouting fretfully in Italian.

"*Basta, e poi basta!*" she screamed. "I've had more than enough. I'm through. I don't give a damn whether you do understand! You never did, anyway. No, no and no! I won't speak bloody English! And keep that woman off me. I'm not her responsibility. I don't want her solicitude. When you started making love to me you never said it was an adoptive daughter you wanted for your barren, cannibal wife!"

"Clara!" Thorne's voice cut in in slow, deliberate English. "I have not understood one word, but I am coming over. You stay right there and don't do anything . . ."

"Jim!" Alice was clearly on another extension. "What's all that screaming about? Do you think she's on drugs?"

"Alice, would you *get off the line* and for once in your sweet life keep your fingers out of mine!"

"Jim, we can't have more than *one* hysteric. The girl needs care. She's obviously trying emotional blackmail on us, but she might call her own bluff and . . . "

The line went dead. The Italian girl must have hung up. Vanni quickly replaced his own receiver. A minute later the phone clicked again. He cautiously began to listen.

"Clara," Thorne was saying. "I want you to promise me to wait where you are. And tell me: have you taken anything?" There was no answer. "Clara!" Jim tried again. "Clara!"

"Jim!" The sound of Alice Thorne's voice was so explosively reproachful in Vanni's ear that he replaced his receiver in a shiver of guilt. For a while he sat watching the telephone which, however, made no further sounds. Minutes later, he heard Thorne run down the driveway to his car.

At six, Mrs. Thorne called Vanni down to have a drink with her. In the middle of it, the phone rang. She got it.

"Well?" she asked. Then, after a pause. "Oh God . . . I'm glad . . . yes. Yes. . . . No, Jim . . . No, *I* think you should both come back right *here*. . . . Of course. . . . *Now!* The hospital what? . . . They won't let her out? . . . Well tomorrow then. Of course. Look, there's no point running away from . . . Immature, that's right! Look, let me talk to her. Clara? Hullo, look, Clara, you *must* trust Jim now. You're in an overwrought state. You need attention. Later, if you . . . Of course we'd *both* love to have you back. Your old room is ready. . . . Don't be childish. . . . Yes. You know we're both fond of you. Good."

Mrs. Thorne sat down, then rose to pour herself another drink. She was on tequila which she drank in small glassfuls, gulping down an entire one at a time after licking some rough kitchen salt off her thumb.

"I suppose", she said to Vanni, "it's obvious what's going on?"

"No."

"Jim's been having an affair with a girl. An Italian." She jerked the salty thumb towards the phone. "That one. I went along with it in the hope that they might work it out of their systems. In fact I'm the one who got her over here. He met her in Italy a year ago. When he came back he was spending more than he earned on long-distance calls and trips back and forth. *That* couldn't go on, so I stepped in. I worked out a plan to get her over here without scandalizing her relatives, set the whole thing up. I offered her a job in the college. She had a room here too which was O.K. since lots of faculty members have student lodgers."

"Yes."

"Well . . ." Mrs. Thorne sighed. "I don't know. It never worked. From the first day she played cat and mouse with him. I don't know did she *sleep* with him, even. . . . And she was very hostile towards *me*. Then they had a row and she moved out. That was before you came. I suppose he's been seeing her. I don't ask. But the latest is she took an overdose of pills and had to have her stomach pumped. She's agreed to come back for a while. Another drink?"

"No, thank you."

"Well, *say* something. You're like *her*! It's scary to have someone suppressing their thoughts all the time."

"Oh . . . I, ah—how old is she?"

"You may well ask. Twenty-three. He's baby-snatching. It's the seven-year itch or something. Multiplied. Besides, he's so insecure. He's always been dependent on me and resents this, so, to prove his manliness, he brings in this young chick."

There was a silence.

"Do you want her back here?" Vanni was practising indiscretion.

"Me? Well—as things *are*: yes. He's got to get her out of his system, so, yes, yes, I do."

"And if she gets—deeper into his system?"

Alice Thorne's lips tightened. "He'll have to be disintoxicated, won't he? I can handle that. I've choreographed the whole *affaire*. Did you know that I've written his books for him? *You* do the research and *I* do the writing. Oh, he sketches in the outline of each chapter, but the actual hoofwork is mine. He has no stamina, you see. No follow through. No *drive!*" She swallowed another tequila and her eyes glowed yellowly. "He's dependent on me," she said. "You'll see!"

She did not join Vanni and her husband for dinner that evening. Thorne fixed hamburgers for the two of them. "Alice is a bit upset," he told Vanni as he patted the red meat into jumbo portions. "She'll be right as rain tomorrow. She's a marvellous woman. What other woman would realize that at my age a man needs a younger woman to arouse him? We have a pretty harmonious relationship going for us. She just doesn't appeal to me *sexually* any more. What do you say to a dash of Tabasco?"

Mrs. Thorne spent the morning out and appeared at luncheon in high good humour. They would be four tonight, she reminded and what about going to Sunset Strip to see some leg shows? "It'll be an experience for Vanni. I'll bet, Vanni, you've never seen burlesque?"

"?"

"Girls in the raw. Exquisite sex objects revolving their well-proportioned meat for your delectation. They strip to the muff in L.A. You can take the news to Lucca."

Vanni quailed. Bars. Drinks. Cost? Signals registered nervously in his head. He'd have to pay one round, maybe more. Soft for himself—lemonade—but the cost? The loss drilled in his pay packet? If there were shows, *Porca Madonna*, it could cost *anything!*

Jim thought Clara might be tired. "And if Vanni doesn't much want to, then . . ."

"Vanni", said Mrs. Thorne, "will love it! Don't tell *me* Italians aren't leg-and-ass watchers! I've watched them watch, charted the ambit of their lusts. But Vanni's been holding out on me, he gives me nothing to go on. We've got to expose him to stimuli so he can give himself away."

"Alice," asked her husband, "what are you high on?"

"Well, *aren't* we perceptive! If you must know I've seen a lawyer."

"I'd rather not know right now."

"Well, you're *going* to know, baby." Mrs. Thorne spoke with exhilaration. "He says that if you want a divorce—*if*, you understand: just an iffy question—then you can certainly get one, but"—speaking in a little girl's voice—"I can make it very expensive for you. Cripplingly expensive. More coffee, Vanni?"

Vanni spent the afternoon at a Japanese movie and walked back at cocktail time, his head full of sabre-work and mystifying cries. The guest was in the drawing-room and hailed him before he had time to back out.

"You're Vanni. I've heard so much about you. I'm Clara."

Ferragamo shoes, silk shirt, skin-texture fine as a greenhouse flower's. How had she wound up here?

"Hullo." Vanni did not like to say he had heard about *her*.

"You're wondering how I came to be here?"

"Yes."

"Game of General Post whereby Italian girls are sent to the U.S., American girls to Italy, Australians to England and so forth. Very 'in' with middle-class parents of marriageable daughters. Just suppose you have a daughter. The young men her age have to be given a few years to make their fortunes but meanwhile you must safeguard her reputation. You can't lock her up the way you could ten years ago—in Italy anyway. What do you do?"

"Tell me."

"Send her—or let her go—abroad. To learn a language, take

a job, study window-dressing. The pretext is secondary. Then she can have a few love affairs safely out of your neighbours' sight and come back in a year or so to marry the boy next door."

"Does the plan never go wrong?"

"Constantly, but neither your neighbours nor their son hear the scandal so what do you care? You don't lose face even if she falls in love—which is the worst thing as it leads to indiscretion."

Vanni grinned. He grinned because he was happy to be talking Italian again after months of being restricted to the blunt, clumsy medium of his English and the even blunter one of Mrs. Thorne's Italian. He grinned too at Clara's ploy. It was a classic one, sombrely companionable: hardly more than a verbal shrug. She had been displaying her lucidity. See, she had been saying, I cannot control what happens to me. I know this and put my pride in knowing it. Her pessimism refreshed him. Pessimism, the counter-virtue to the "drive" animating Alice Thorne, was his own guiding principle and Anna's too. In its orbit came satellite qualities of proven use in Lucca but perhaps less handy here: suspicion, thrift, dilatoriness, deviousness and a tendency to restrict loyalties. He wondered how this girl would make out in her set-to with Mrs. Thorne.

"I hear we're going out this evening."

"Would you have any idea", Vanni nerved himself to ask, "what drinks cost in a night-club?"

The girl shrugged. "No. Don't you pay, anyway. Why should you? *They*'ll drink ten times more than you and tomorrow nobody will remember who picked up the tab. Besides, Jim won't let you." She laughed in triumph. It was a rich caress of a name in her mouth: D Jimm.

When the Thornes came in, talk shifted to English. Thorne, closely shaven and wearing a business suit, had toned himself down to the point of near invisibility. He moved silently across the carpeted floor, pouring drinks, lighting cigarettes, responding when directly addressed, then seeming to lapse into a dream. The girl was quiet too. But this self-effacement—as with the celebrants of religious ceremonies—only intensified one's awareness of an impalpable element, a power connecting them as they sat, two magnetic poles, in different corners of the room.

They had been to five clubs. Vanni had stoically paid the first round of drinks. He was unsure how much it had set him back as he had let Thorne fish the bills from his wallet. He was drinking tonic water and was sober although slightly sick. Everywhere they went Mrs. Thorne managed to get a table by the stage, and clapped more loudly than anyone else in the club. Vanni trembled lest one of the strippers should be encouraged to come over and say something incomprehensible to him or run her panties under his nose. This fear robbed the evening of all erotic stimulus.

"This", Clara remarked, "is the twenty-second woman we have seen strip. I've been counting. If one had three breasts, I might just revive a little interest."

"*Vanni*'s loving it," said Mrs. Thorne. She had been keeping up this fiction and had written down the name of every club they had been to so that he could impress his Lucchesi friends with the list. "Hey, isn't *this* the place they allow you up on the stage to participate?" She turned to joke with a half-naked waitress. Vanni was chill with fear. He thought he might be her elected butt for the evening, a lightning conductor or clown whose discomfort would camouflage what was going on between Jim and the girl.

"Are you all right?" It was Clara whispering in Italian. "You look green!"

"It's close in here."

"Why don't we leave?" Clara suggested. "Vanni's tired and so am I."

"Don't give me that! Vanni's not a party-pooper. He's going to *participate* in a moment, aren't you, Vanni?" Mrs. Thorne's noisiness attracted attention to their table. The stripper—she had a blue light apparently buried in her vulva—approached crabwise, contorting her body so that her head hung to the backs of her knees. The blue light, like a displaced cyclopic eye between the advancing knee-caps, mesmerized him. He began to sweat, shrinking and—most inappropriately and involuntarily—wriggling in—Oh God—time to the music. But all eyes were not, as he had supposed, on himself. They were on the chair beside him. Clara was standing on it and had taken off her blouse.

"All right then, let's all participate," she called. "Let's all strip. Come on everybody. This other stuff is sick."

She took her brassière off, and her breasts—they were like home-grown fruit compared to the exotic bulbs on the strippers—looked touchingly vulnerable and more naked than anything seen all evening.

Someone clapped and a girl at another table began to unzip her dress. Simultaneously, a man with a managerial air approached with the bouncer. Thorne stood up.

"O.K., we're leaving."

Their coats were produced and in under a minute they were outside on the pavement. Alice Thorne for once was speechless.

Back at the house, Vanni, from his own room, heard his host's footsteps in the corridor, a stealthy twisting of Clara's doorknob and the sounds of retreat. He fell asleep but was awakened several hours later by further whispered beseeching. The next night he thought he heard the sounds again.

On Saturday, Mrs. Thorne proposed another evening on the town but Vanni refused to go. The others went without him. At 1 a.m. by his bedside clock he awoke to scuffling sounds and raised voices. There was a bang and the grating of a lock in Clara's door. Then door-thumping. "Let me in!" shouted Thorne's voice. "Clara, open up!" Moments later the front door banged and there was a crash of glass outside Clara's window followed by a padding of feet. Vanni's door was flung open. It was Clara in her nightgown.

"Vanni, help me. Jim's gone berserk!"

Mrs. Thorne's door opened and *she* appeared also in night attire: a candy-pink-and-yellow baby-doll smock which, leaving her thighs bare, made her look like a deteriorated infant: the wizened fifth, say, of a set of quins which survives just long enough to be photographed for the evening papers. "What is it, Clara?" she asked.

Clara flinched. "I'm sorry, Alice, but Jim's had too much to drink. He put his fist through the glass of my window. There's blood on the window-sill. He may be hurt."

"Where is he now?"

"In the garden. I think he locked himself out."

Mrs. Thorne walked to the front door, fixed a chain on it and shot two bolts. "Well, he's locked out now," she said. "I locked the back door earlier."

"But his hand?"

"He won't bleed to death," said his wife. "Better let him cool off." Her lips were tightly drawn. "He couldn't get in your window anyway," she said. "They're all barred. If he's cold he can go to a motel. Would either of you like cocoa? No? Well, my head's worse. See you in the morning."

She left.

"Oh Lord," said Clara. "Come and have a drink with me, Vanni."

He followed her into the drawing-room.

"Pull the curtains," she whispered.

"We can't keep him out of his own house, can we?"

"It's not us. It's Alice." She gave a quick sour laugh. "And it's her house."

"In law, I don't think, even a wife . . . but then American law may be different?"

"Law? You, don't think he'd call the *police*?"

Vanni poured two drinks. "Why don't you sleep with him?" he astonished himself by asking. His voice was testy.

"Under her roof? That's what she wants: to pimp for me. For him—well, whichever it is."

"Then why come here?"

"He asked me. He promised he'd ask her for a divorce. It was all to be clarified—but she winds him round her finger. This is the second time he's gone back on a promise, on a major promise. He reneges on little ones all the time. All year it's been like this: on; off; on; off. She never says 'no' to begin with, but then, slowly, she makes difficulties, threats. . . . She frightens him. The money is hers. The house too. She could get him fired from his job. . . ."

There was a bang on the front door. Clara clutched Vanni. "Don't answer."

Vanni put out the light. "Shshsh!"

They sat in the dark. Footsteps crunched away from the front of the house. Clara began to whisper: "I hate doing this to him, Vanni. Look, I'm in love with the man. I don't want to play it this way. I *want* to sleep with him, but—well, *Oddio*, it's indecent, obscene. She's always there. She practically tucks us into bed together. And it's not that *he's* a weakling. It's *she* who is a monster. Really. She uses everyone. She uses you. Did you know she's persuaded him that *you* fancy her? I'll bet you didn't. He thinks you're dying with lust for her but too shy to do anything about it. She calls you 'Vespone or the dumb waiter'. After some character in a play."

"An opera."

"You know it? I *am* turning into a bitch, telling you that. I'm sorry."

The side-door bell rang. Brrrrrrrrrrrrrrrrr!

"I'd go to a hotel—but how can I? He's out there. Berserk. And she . . ."

Another ring: longer this time.

"Let's go into my bedroom. It's safer. There's a lock. Will you come and close my blind?"

Brrrrrrrrrrrrrrrrrr!

Following her, Vanni felt his shoe grind glass into the carpet pile. Like a virus, the other man's passion fumed around the house. Clara's scent was behind him as he fixed the blind. Her hair brushed his cheek.

"Kiss me."

"What are you up to?"

"Oh, Vanni, we both need it. It'll do nobody any harm and us good. Come on. Oh, come *on*, Vanni. Your wife's in Lucca. Jim won't know and it'll keep me sane—keep me from charging round inside the house the way he's doing outside. Keep you from assaulting la Thorne!" She laughed. Her teeth glistened at him and her soft, flower-like face glowed furrily in the lamplight. "Mmmh?" She smiled, coquetted, making fun of her own offer even as she made it. Vanni thought of a pretty nursemaid playfully teasing a child. "You know you want to, Vanni!"

"No."

"Liar."

He shrugged angrily and turned his back on her.

"All right," he heard, "I'm sorry. *Come non detto*. O.K.?"

"I've fixed your blind."

"Well that's something. . . . Good night, Vanni. Sweet dreams."

He walked out of her door, aware of the punctilious set of his shoulders and the unfair fact that he had been dealt another ridiculous role: sidekick-who-refuses-to-horn-in-on-hero's-preserves. Though what—Vanni swore to himself—was heroic about Thorne he failed to see. Why was Thorne dashing because he lusted and Vanni dull because he did not? Hollywood ethics, he thought sourly: vitality equals virility equals lust and the "vir" had been removed from "virtue". He thought with displeasure of the day when Alice Thorne's yellow-clawed hand had disdainfully landed on his fly. Her psychological jargon clawed as destructively at any manifestation of life which seemed more complex than an appetite. What right had she to despise him and call him names? Because he ate her bread? Because he was mild, polite, cautious with money? Ah yes, *money* was the sap of virility. Vanni paused in the bathroom to throw water on his face. He was upset. His bodily humours were in an uproar. He imagined them as ancient medicine had: black bile, yellow bile and phlegm ebbing and washing tidally through his organism, upsetting its careful balance. Clara—that child—*had* upset him, arousing in him a doubt and sort of lust for lust. Reminding him of areas of himself usually kept battened down, she had raised the worst question: was there anything there to batten? She and the Thornes were spoilt, to be sure, over-indulged. But hadn't a worse kind of spoiling been drying the pith out of Vanni Moncini since—*Porca Madonna*, he refused to think since when: the spoiling that overtakes produce kept too long unused? Anna and he spent their energies contriving and surviving. With four children and no job, the odds were against them, for they belonged to the lower-middle class: that glamourless social caste which, defended by neither Left nor Right, puts its trust in the old patriarchal virtues, and is out of step with the rest of society. Anna would sit up until midnight for a week to make herself a silk dress so as to cut a decent figure. Mrs. Thorne, who could have charged ten silk dresses at Magnins's, preferred jeans. But why was *she* right? Anna looked better. Anna, Vanni told himself sorrowfully, had spent as much energy and ingenuity on keeping herself and her children decent in the last ten years as three American presidents on their failure to destroy Vietnam.

But, meanwhile, where had pleasure gone? Play? Passion? Youth?

The mirror in Vanni's bedroom packaged a shopkeeper's face: the face he had turned on Clara. The face that refuses credit, licks its thumb the better to turn greasy pages, distrusts impulse, takes no risk. Walking right up to it, Vanni bared his teeth. "Clerk! *Bottegaio!*" He wriggled his ears. "Sucker!" He stuck out his tongue. Seen so close up, it was surprisingly wet and fleshy. It should have belonged to those other three greedy grabbers of the immediate. He stared with fascination at the spry, muscular organ, so live, so variegated and three dimensional. Glandular, tentacular. It reminded him of sea beasts. He wriggled it about, bent and stretched it, staring into its rivulets and medusoid buds. *La lingua non ha osso, ma rompe il dosso!* He had, he thought with amusement, as good a tongue as anyone. His carnal equipment was in good order. He began to laugh. What a farce all the same! Two-in-the-morning thoughts! Who was perfect, after all? Who happy? Not that silly child nor the poor wound-up bastard charging round the house nor that other one in bed with her psychology texts! They weren't even *good* at grabbing the immediate. The efficient grabber of it was himself: Vanni Moncini, thrifty Tuscan and man of honour who would return with money in mitt to wife and children, make a down payment on a house and sail through the English-language part of the archivists' exam—the rest of it was no trouble. In a few months he would be an archivist. It was a snug job with a pension. Social Security benefits and all-but-free season tickets on the National Railways. On Sundays he could take his family to Viareggio. . . .

There was a knock on the door. "Vanni, did I hear you laughing? Look, may I come in? I'm nervous. Please let me stay."

He opened the door for her. She slunk through. She was drooping like a wet bird and her eyes were puffy.

"What's the matter now, Clara?"

"Oh, I'm being weak. I'm sorry. I'm sorry for a while ago too. I'm losing control I think. I was thinking just now—oh, about how pointless it is my having a trial of strength with *her*. I mean, she never lets go, does she. She always wins. Everyone gives in to her. Jim will too and I'll lose him. Maybe I should spare everyone the fuss and give in now?"

"You weren't", Vanni remembered, "thinking of taking another overdose?"

"I haven't got any more."

"Couldn't you and he go away somewhere? Off her ground."

Clara drooped even more. "She can get him fired for moral turpitude."

"Did you mean to kill yourself", he asked, "when you took those pills?"

"I don't know." She shrugged. "Maybe it was strategy? Maybe exhaustion? I was alone in a nasty little room in Brentwood and I got depressed." She made a gesture of fatigue, fatalism, a familiar gesture to Vanni who suddenly thought, seeing her hunched up in his armchair, her knees under her chin, her long lawn nightdress with smocking on the chest and her tear-puffed face, that one of his own daughters might look—live?—like this in a few years from now.

"If we do *anything* . . . she can, well, blackmail him really: demand money. He owes her more than he's got. We must lie low."

"Lie low! *Eh già!*"

The words, components of a grubby survival-code for underdogs, aroused a Pavlovian response. Vanni nodded. Resignation settled into the niche between his shoulder-blades.

"Yes!"

Why. Yes? Irritably, he twitched, angered by the ease with which their two minds slid on to servile tracks. Clara aged before his eyes. "*Porca mattinata*, Clara, don't you know enough to go after what you want? Single-mindedly! Seize! Steal if you have to. Love! Laugh! That's what freedom's for. Do what you want *if* you want—and if you don't want then what in God's name are you doing here? Trying to drive that unfortunate man into a mental institution? Poor bastard! To be caught between that monster and a . . . Look, when you're my wife's age and saddled with four kids will be time enough to start resigning yourself!"

With something close to horror, Clara stared. "But what . . . can *I* do?"

"Go out to him now! Leave with him. Sod the consequences." Persuaded—and astounded—by the conviction in his voice, Vanni propelled her out of his room and down the corridor. As they passed the hall closet, he unhooked a coat and put it round her shoulders, guided her through the dark kitchen, shot the bolts and turned the key in the back-door lock. "Some of us are stuck, tied by the leg by responsibilities . . . but you, Clara . . ." Tired of argument, he pointed into the leafy blackness of the garden. God-the-Father on a reversed reel, he motioned her towards transgression, roared and pointed: "Go!"

She went. Hearing an answering rustle from among the camellia bushes, Vanni shut the door. A sound of something spattering on to the floor made him turn.

Alice Thorne was leaning against the refrigerator less than six feet away from him. Urine poured down her bare legs, hitting the linoleum with a slap, then sputtering outwards in a pale, brilliant pool. As she peed, the pool spread across the dark floor, engulfing it in reflections from the garden lighting which Thorne must have turned on. The smell was strong. Alice's face, caught in the same light, was as rigid as her body. Finished, she turned and walked out of the kitchen. She was still wearing the ridiculous baby-doll night-dress but no longer struck Vanni as ridiculous. She had acquired the dignity of a victim. Dodging the flood, Vanni followed her as far as a bathroom door which she had imperfectly closed behind her. Through it came sounds of water and steam. She had not turned on the light.

"Alice!"

No answer.

"Alice, are you all right?"

Nothing.

Vanni pushed the door. "I'm coming in."

"No light! I don't want light."

"All right." He stepped inside the door and stood, sniffing and trying to see. "You're not doing . . . anything? Are you?"

"Cutting my veins?" Her laugh was hoarse. "That's not my act. That's her act. Pills she used. Pretty, pastel pills. Aroused pity. Wouldn't for me. I'm the monster."

"Alice . . ."

"Shit, Vanni, I'm *washing*. That's all."

"You're shaking. Here. Is this a bathrobe? Step out and I'll dry you. Come on. Give me your hand."

"I don't need . . ."

"You do. Come on."

He felt her thin shoulders through the terry-towelling. "That's right," he rubbed her through the stuff, then guided her, groping with one hand for furniture, towards her own room. "Lie down," he told her. "Give me the robe. It's wet. I'll get you a drink."

"No light. Not here. Put on the corridor light. That'll be enough."

From the bar, he heard her shout: "Whiskey, Vanni. Neat. Fill the glass."

He brought it back to her and she gulped half it down at once.

"O.K. Florence Nightingale," she said. "You can go now."

"Can't I stay? I poured myself a drink, too."

She shrugged. "I guess any scrap of human solidarity I could get this minute would be welcome. But I'm not sick and I don't aim to be your good turn for the year, get it? I've not yet seen any spontaneous good feeling come from you to me—though you owe me some. If I brought you out here, got you a job, opened my house to you and helped you with your English, it wasn't because I was after your body. You *will* grant that? I just thought it would be a decent thing to do. I saw you trapped and tried to help. And you—just now you told that girl I was a monster. Why?"

There was a pause which Vanni felt unable to break. After some moments, Alice spoke again.

"Yeah, well I guess for an Italian a homely woman has to be just that: a monster. The body is all—or rather the face because, as it happens, my body's O.K. Not monstrous. Not by any standards. No, sir." She finished the glass. "More," she commanded. Vanni left and came back with the bottle. She filled her glass. "What I'm getting at is your materialism. For you, what you can see and touch is all. The lot. Period. St. Theresa's spirit could inhabit my body and *you'd* call her a monster. Then you say *Americans* are materialists!"

"Alice, please!" Vanni was overwhelmed. "You must let me defend myself. I never mentioned your body, your ... anything like that. It's your own obsession speaking. . . . All right, I did use the word 'monster'. But I meant that you seemed to have paralyzed Jim's *will*. That you take all his decisions for him."

"And that's not feminine, right? But, baby, you can't play the little old feminine game when you look like I do. Even supposing you *wanted* to play that goddam . . . ah shit. Look, I'm collapsing again. Where are the Kleenex? Look, go *away*, Vanni, will you."

"Please let me stay."

"You're *on her side!*"

"No."

"Haha!"

"I'm on nobody's side!"

"Well that," Alice's voice cut, sharp as a ventriloquist's across her own laughter, "Vanni Moncini, is where you give yourself away! You're on nobody's side but your own."

"Alice, you're excited, maybe you'd better rest?"

"I can *talk*, can't I? In my own room in my own house? Talk doesn't affect you, does it? You're zipped up too tight to be affected: wallet, mind, and every aperture zipped tight as a bull's ass in fly-time! For all *you* care we can all and every one of us go and jump in the ocean or—to quote a limey I once knew—sod each other up and down the flag-pole. 'Sod me up and down the flag-pole,' he used to say. It's *funny*, Vanni! Can't you even crack a grin? No? O.K., you're saving your laughs, too, for the folks back home. Right? Right. But just remember: we gave you a chance here you never got back in Lucca. *Gave* it, mind. You didn't hold us up. Though I guess *that* is how you've set things up in your own mind. This, you think, is the material Paradise full of material loot for the taking and the bringing home. You're a Manichee, Vanni. You divide the world into spirit and matter and allot the spirit to your own tribe. So-o-o, if one of us, Jim, shall we say, is drawn to one of you—Clara—this leaning of his is a leaning towards the spiritual and should be encouraged! Me, I stand for matter and homely matter at that. How can I win? The 'monster', the base materialist. But I'm less materialistic than you. I don't care about objects. Look."

She picked up a miniature colour television set which she kept on her bedside table.

"*This* cost $400 at Bullock's," she said, and smashed it to the floor. The floor was carpeted and the set did not break. She smashed it down again, hitting the corner of a bureau so that the screen split. She bent to pick it up and was on the point of hurling it down once more when Vanni caught her wrists.

"Stop!"

In their struggle she fell across the bed and he across her. The television slid gently on to the carpet. Alice Thorne thrust her knee painfully into Vanni's groin. He yelped.

"*Stronza!*"

He banged her head against the wall. "There's a devil in you!"

"Manichee!" Again she kneed him painfully.

"Bitch!"

"You think", she panted, "you're su-superior, but, ah, you're afraid—afraid to get to know us in case you find out different!

Why didn't you ever visit the Music Center? The galleries?"

"I can't drive. I couldn't get there."

"Wouldn't learn!"

"No money!"

"You're afraid!" She bit him.

While they were struggling and shouting, she—or was it he? He couldn't afterwards be sure—had unbuttoned him and one sinewy hand started kneading his penis. He shoved it into her and as he moved it in and out was aware that she was still panting out talk which he sometimes managed to gag.

"Grease-servile immigrants used to be," she panted. "But you—tried to protect yourself—wouldn't comm-communicate. Pride," she said, squeezing his testicles.

"Stop!" he shouted and drove into her.

"Grease," she shouted.

"It's yours."

"I'm the monster. I'll devour you."

"Shut up," whispered Vanni, "marvellous monster."

Vanni had a month left before leaving. He spent it playing house with Alice Thorne, who taught him to drive and let him ferry her all over the city to restaurants where they tried Mexican and Chinese and Hawaiian food. When Vanni confessed this to be a culture shock, she insisted on buying Italian ingredients and taking them home to attempt a few Tuscan dishes. He, who had never cooked himself, had exigent theories about the art and was shocked and indeed disappointed to find her ingenuity up to this.

"Oh, I can cook if I want," she said carelessly, "I just don't care to most of the time. I take short-cuts if I can. There's no real virtue in a lot of the old laborious ways. They just made women feel they were earning their keep."

They took time off to drive up the coast and into the desert and one day she took him in her open sports car down the blowy, sunny, looping highways to Marine Land, where they watched whales and dolphins leap astounding vertical leaps while trainers accompanied the performance with inane patter and defiled the mythic beasts with waterproof baseball caps. The clash on that shore between classic memories and KABC voices grinding their spiel mirrored the confusion in Vanni's feelings. Alice, it seemed to him, had the steely grace of the dolphins, their power and often their kitschy defenceless awfulness as when they obeyed their trainer's signal to waddle on their tails across the water-surface, nuzzling some incongruous object such as an inflated Thanksgiving pumpkin. On the whole, he decided that Alice and the dolphins could, with some retention of dignity, survive the slapstick situations which seemed to arise in this country whereas he, Vanni, probably could not.

About a week before he was due to fly home, Alice told him:

"Jim and the girl are arriving tonight. I just got a telegram."

"Oh. I see."

"You don't need to feel embarrassed. Jim won't be."

"Mmm. Why do you suppose they are coming back?"

"I guess they reached the end of their road."

Vanni *was* embarrassed at being found in his new situation by the other two. It was so unsurprising, such a foregone conclusion. He had, he supposed now—anyway *they* would now suppose he had—been teetering for months on the edge of it, as a golf-ball putted to the edge of the hole can teeter before sinking. He greeted Clara, who came straight to his room, with some discomfort. But she was thinking about herself:

"I didn't bring it off!"

Almost immediately she was in tears and emitting her monotone supplicant's cry: cry of the defenceless herbivore. Doe? Rabbit? Mouse? Her lips nuzzled air and breast heaved as she gave the signals with which weak animals conciliate the strong of their own species. This, Vanni supposed, classed *him* as buck rabbit or dominant mouse. A stag perhaps? She begged advice, was at the end of her tether. Return here was recognizable defeat.

"I *pleaded* with Jim. I can't understand—and that's the worst part—the pull she has over him. I *know* he loves me. I know it. It isn't just sex. We're alike. We laugh at the same things. I was reading his books and he kept saying how well I understood them. This time, Vanni, I thought it was going to be all right. I had him, as you said, 'off her ground'. And then . . . Vanni, what can I do?"

So how had Vanni got himself *in loco parentis sacerdotisque* to Clara? Was it because he, an evil counsellor, had used her to get Jim off the premises so as to make way for his own friskings? Deliberately? Subconsciously? Shit no! He dismissed an Alice thought-pattern with an Alice expletive: shit. Well then? Or sent her ahead of himself to test the fires of extra-conjugal passion? She had come back singed.

"Help me, Vanni."

Her shaking shoulders implored a brotherly/fatherly/loverly caress. Vanni gagged at the responsibility. Jim, it occurred to him, might too.

"Clara," he hesitated then plunged. "You'd better give up. I'm sorry. It *was* worth a try but the try hasn't come off." Or was he wrong again? No. "*Senti*, Clara. I've come to know Alice better. . . ."

She looked at him, slowly—he saw this happen—grasping the fact that events unconnected with herself might yet affect her. "You . . . and she?"

"Yes. It's no good, Clara."

"You must be joking. You advised me to go with him. I love him, Vanni."

"Love", Vanni shrugged, "is very nice, Clara, but you have to earn it. It earns nothing itself."

"*He* loves *me*."

Her monotone cry!

"You *said* . . ." she accused.

"I'll rot in hell for giving bad advice."

". . . she was a *monster*. You said . . ."

"I did. I know." She *was*, moreover: a Chimera, Vanni decided, that blend of lion, goat and serpent. She had their qualities. Clara had . . . a kitten's. The match was unthinkable: a butchery. Clara's obtuse, refusing face annoyed him. "You haven't a hope!"

"You *said* that. Why? What's so great about her?"

"She's the anti-woman: not devious, not patient, not pretty, not emotional really. She's as reliable as . . . a computer. Jim knows he can always rely on her. *You* would be relying on *him*."

"She's so awful. Even her voice is awful!" Clara gave a raucous, nasal imitation of it: "Weyweywey!"

Extreme, Vanni thought, like a coloratura's pitch. Alice throve on third-act operatic emotion which would burn Clara up—or Vanni.

"She's too much for either of us, Clara."

"Jim . . ."

"Jim's inured, addicted. He'll always remember you, but don't ask him for permanence. You're a marvellous, sexy woman, Clara! Lots of men will want you, love you, marry you, but . . ." Vanni crooned out the reassurance, the caressing words that Clara needed, stroked her hair, let her cry. She would come back with him. He would deliver her home. Maybe Alice had even counted on this? The economy of her calculation took his breath away. Old serpentine Chimera. To think he had once feared he was not paying his way! But generous too: gave as much as she took and took what she wanted against all odds. Had she not—he chuckled inwardly while continuing to comfort Clara—got himself, Vanni, the tightest of the uptight to, as she would have said "participate"? Accomplished puppet-mistress! Teleguided, his hand stroked Clara's wrist. It was frail and translucent as a begonia stem. "You're young," he reminded her. "Write it off to experience. A good experience, a wisening one. You'll be better off in Italy. The going's too hard for you here, Clara."

Clara, sobbing now with the gusty wildness of a child, muttered that she hated this country: "Crude," she panted, "horrible, tough!"

Vanni could feel the pulsing throb of her belly warm against his thigh. Again, he was reminded of a kitten. "Oh," he said vaguely, for a slow tide of sensuality was blurring his thought processes, "it's not quite like that. When we go back, people will ask us about this country and we won't know what to say. It's hard to sum up . . . Clara. . . ."

Lots of Ghastlies

Her mother's now was a triple-layered face: icing-bright make-up dabs bobbed, brave as bunting, upon tides of fat and, somewhere beneath, foundered the shrewd, pretty, barfly's features. Only the Cupid's-bow lips were still the same: eager and shiny as when they used to kiss Priss quick, distracted good-nights. ("Comi-i-ing, you lot! Won't be a sec! Just gotta say good-night to the . . . Be a good girl now, Priss. Say your prayers. Sleep tight!" And out of the door to the gang in the car, leaving behind her a waft of gin-and-lime and Amour-Amour.) She'd had to go on the wagon years ago.

"This neon's awful," said Priss with depression.

"Oh?" said her mother. "Everyone has it for the kitchen. What do they use in Italy?"

"This, too, I expect. I mean it's hard on the face."

Her mother looked at her. "It's true you've gone off," she said. "Since—how long since you were here? Four years? Five?"

"Three and a half," said Priss. "*Because* I was out of the country."

"Well, whatever life you've been leading, it's aged you. A little flesh keeps the skin smooth after thirty. You've got bags under your eyes." The glance slid downward. "What happened to your bust?"

"Busts are *Out*."

Her mother's eye continued to descend and reached the bowl in which Priss was stirring eggs. "What", her voice kited up, then was controlled, "are you doing with ALL those eggs? THREE?"

"Making mayonnaise for supper. I saw you had salad in the fridge and Daddy's always liked mayonnaise."

"With THREE eggs! Are you MAD?"

In a storm, the old groove-lines in her mother's face could not control the new yeastiness. This was a storm. Her flesh bubbled. She seized the bowl from Priss but then did not know what to do with it. She considered the vulnerable, quaking yolks, which could not now be restored to their shells, and paused.

"Goodness, I'll pay you for them if you like!"

"Pay! That's a nice one! Ha! From you!"

"Oh . . ."

"The way you paid back the hundred pounds I sent you to get married with!"

"Ten years ago, for God's sake!"

"Stop swearing! And did you get married? I suppose you'd never expected to? Pay—you may live in luxury with your rich friends. Mayonnaise, caviar no doubt. . . . You have the tastes. . . . Eggs cost . . ."

"*Mother!*"

"Don't address me in that tone. You're irresponsible. You couldn't even keep your own child—what did happen to her?"

"Peregrine? She's been adopted. You won't be asked to lay out anything for her."

"Poor child. . . ." Her mother sniffled. "I suppose I'll never see her now. . . ."

"You never wanted to before. . . ."

Her mother had seen something in the sink. "The WHITES!" she shouted. "You threw them away! THREE whites! Down the drain!"

The sniffles had turned to sobs. Her mother let herself fall on to a hard-backed kitchen chair. "It's so typical," she wailed. "I don't know. . . . I've always wanted things to be nice between us. . . ."

Priss took off her apron and walked back to the living-room. Her father cocked an eye up from the television.

He whispered: "A little drinky?"

"Should you?"

He closed the eye. He was no older than Bandino, who still zipped around Europe in racing cars and could polish off a magnum of champagne any night of the week. *Or* topple a bird when Priss's back was turned. She filled two glasses. Her father grinned, then winked again. "Bottoms up!" His eye boomeranged back to the TV programme: a cricket match. There was a bounce in him still. He'd always been a great one for ball games: rugby, golf, even croquet. She remembered grassy afternoons and a triumphant flow of liquor as he whisked balls through hoops and into holes. "Not bad, what? Got to keep my end up with you chaps!" A ricocheting laugh. He'd been a bookie, though she told Bandino and all her London friends that he was "an Army man". They imagined a tight-lipped officer whose behaviour when she'd first slipped from the path of virtue precluded her return to it. ("Brought up strictly, kicked over the traces . . ." It was neat and satisfying. Like his wink.) In fact, she couldn't remember his behaviour. There hadn't been any. He had been indifferent, absorbed in her mother who, then as now, had wept over things turning out less nicely than she had anticipated. Her maternal tears flowed with the ease of juice from a plastic lemon. She had been a plucked-browed beauty, toast of the golf club, swaying in the sun on ginny dappled afternoons as he cocked his shots. Plip! Plop! "A neat poke! Cheers!"

And now he sits glued to the telly while I cavort around Europe with old Bandino. I should get him a girl. One of my friends. Miranda, perhaps, or even Catherine. He has charm and an older man makes you feel young. Better to be young flesh for someone else than to be on the prowl for it. I mean for a woman. At thirty-two one is in between. Poor Daddy watching his little screen: a shrunken world. He used to be such a great juicy man, all strawberry and ginger colours. He had a sweet smile as if his teeth were coloured by a film of honey. But rarely for me: a lanky sprat in convent uniform. How old was I—eleven?—the Sunday morning I went into their bed-room. The char hadn't come for some reason and I had been waiting for my breakfast for hours. There was a powerful shaft of sunlight coming through the curtains on to the bed and I saw them doing something astonishing—I hadn't the faintest idea what. Indeed, I forgot about it for years. What I remembered was *his* fury and the way he leaped up, carelessly naked, pink and quivering with rage, to order me out of their room. "Out!" A thunderclap. Rigid pointing finger. A hairy, gold-glinting God-the-Father condemning curiosity, when all I'd wanted was my breakfast and not to be left alone so long in my room. "Your room!" he shouted. "Go to your room!" And off I slunk, wrapped in my Teddy-bear dressing-gown and not understanding a thing.

"Prissy!"

He was looking at her from under still-ginger brows. "Another gin?"

"If *you* do."

He held up the bottle in a way she had seen her mother do, tracing the liquid-line with a finger-nail.

"She marks it," he murmured.

Oh, Lord! Why? His liver? But we all have livers. Bandino has. He takes pills and visits the fashionable spas but drinks like a fish. Says he wants to go out with a bang. Or—could it be because I was coming? I, with my baggy eyes and indeterminate status.

"Better keep the bottle out of sight while she's around, dear!"

So they think I'm a lush! And irresponsible. I brought a daughter into the world and don't devote myself to her! *She'd* like to see me tied down among nappies, feed-bottles, potties, and plastic teething things! Oh, yes. Revenge. A lousy mother she was, too! Peregrine has a nice adoptive one: broody and barren. Big-bosomy Sarah, born to the role. One should always have I.B.M.-linked mother teams: "Sexy, fertile producer seeks good child-rearer." Peregrine shall judge. No, she shall not. She'll probably grow up to be something depressing like a lady don when I've joined the Light Brigade of old English bags

one sees propped about the gaming tables in places like Deau-
ville, getting my last chancy pleasures in a game of chemmy.
"Oh, my mama", she'll say of me with a giggle, "is such a
character. . . ." Meanwhile, I'll have a wanton drink with my
treacherous old Dad.

She poured him a stiff one. He examined it with some alarm.

"Come on, Daddy! Never say die!"

His laugh again. Golden hairs on the hand that tapped her
knee.

"You're a bad lot, Prissy."

If I weren't his daughter now he'd pinch my bottom. If I
were just some still-youngish bird. As I am: not quite a boiler
yet, for all my eye-bags. I can look damn well if I go off the
liquor for a week or two, or even if I don't, I can look damn
well with the proper make-up and hair-do. God, though, I used
to be so marvellous-looking *all* the time and now. . . . Oh, that
night last April when Peregrine's father—when *Paul*—turned
up at a dinner-party and I introduced him to Bandino! I had
been looking forward to seeing him again, even though he did
behave like a bastard, and I wanted to let him see I was with
someone as grand as he—he always was a snob—and to let
Bandino meet him for the same reason. I knew Paul's wife
would be there but I felt no interest. She had been the reason
Paul wouldn't acknowledge Peregrine, but that was water
under the bridge and wives—"*Mesdames les légitimes*", as that
girl from Lyons, what was her name, used to call them—are
better not thought about. Paul had been crazy about me. Everyone said so, and said that *if* that sort of provincial aristocrat
ever did break loose, he would have for me. In our story I was
the beautiful and the damned so, by all the rules, she must be
a homely country mouse, mustn't she? And then . . . this mag-
nificent brilliant bird appeared—oh, an apparition—in an
Ungaro dress, looking as though every bit of her had been put
together by hand: a unique, *hors série*, top-designer creation;
clever, too, speaking four or five languages—it was that sort
of dinner—and looking ten years younger than me. I saw
Bandino's eyes rolling toward her and Paul's shock at the sight
of drooping me. Oh, yes! "*Ou sont nos amoureuses?/Elles sont au*

tombeau.|Elles sont plus heureuses|Dans un séjour plus beau. . . ."
A convenient arrangement. *I* would have liked to have been in the *tombeau* that evening and I felt Paul would have preferred me there, too. A painful session. Lots of ghastlies. Oh, well.

"A penny for them, Priss?"

"They're not worth it."

"Drink up," invited her father surprisingly. "A little of what you fancy", he put on a comic accent, "does you good!"

Ha! The liquor is warming him, bringing *him* back from the tomb. That's what he needs more of. Better to die roaring than whining. Think of the aids and props Paul and Bandino have: tapestried houses, dogs, pistols, Jaguars, birds. Daddy has to make do with his telly. And *she* goes berserk over the loss of three egg whites. If I touched him now—as she did then—would he revive completely?

Her mother brought in an unnecessarily heavy tray, struggling. They both leaped.

"Mother, you should have called. Let me take it."

"Well, if you want to!" Relinquishing it without grace: "Hardly worth it at this point."

She'd cooked, or rather fixed, a meal: beans on toast, sausages, beer. No sign of the mayonnaise. No salad. A deliberately depressing, austerity meal. As if to remind Priss what she had come from and let her not forget it: poor-but-honest; plain-and-decent. Untrue. All those golf and tennis clubs must have cost a packet. Not to mention the liquor. In the old bookie and nookie days when Priss was packed off to boarding-school, insulated in coarse woollen underwear, *she*'d had it good. Priss didn't grudge it to her. She *wanted* her to have it good, for God's sake.

"I'm afraid this is dull fare for Priss!" Her mother cast her into the semi-absence of the third person.

Did they *like* her visiting? They groused when she stayed away but perhaps preferred their grouse? Or were they pleased but had forgotten how to show it?

"But I *adore* bangers!" she said. Which sounded—Jesus!

"How long can you stay?" her mother asked.

Play this by ear! Bandino was supposedly in Scotland with

people who, knowing his wife, could not sanction Priss. Shooting birds. Not his favourite activity with birds, though he was capable even of that! Anyway, he was to pick her up on Tuesday at the local town where he had dropped her off today. But —should she stay here till Tuesday?

"I'm afraid I upset your routine."

"Oh, don't consider *us*!" said her mother.

"We see so little of you," said her father.

Now that was warm! Wasn't it? It was.

"Darlings," said she. It wasn't their sort of word but it was *her* sort and she felt spontaneous suddenly. Better display this surge of affection before it ebbed. "*Darlings!* It is super to be with you a bit and you are looking marvellous. Both of you!" she squeezed his wrist and knew she should do something of the same sort to her mother, too; but her mother was on her left—a sluggish side of her—and the bread-board had got in between, and her mother's right hand was defensively busy with food, so she didn't. Damn!

He raised his tankard and crinkled his eyes at her over the rim.

I really like Englishmen best: that restrained humour of theirs as they play you along, casting slowly like sensual fishermen. They can seethe and steam, too. Only they have no sex myth, which is a pity. I mean, vim for vim, it's often their picture of themselves as cocks that keeps men going. Look at Bandino. He talks much more than he performs nowadays. But he talks very well. And his seductions are mostly for show.

Did Daddy, I wonder, ever step out on my mother?

"To us," said her father, drinking his beer.

Her mother made a little stabbing movement with her glass. She couldn't drink now because of her diabetes. This time Priss caught her hand as she put it down. Her mother let her hand be held, then relinquished. It was an inconclusive gesture.

But I would like, thought Priss, to be warm with her.

She helped her father wash up. "Why don't we nip out to the local?" she suggested. "When we finish this."

Her father looked worried. "Your mother", he reminded her, "can't drink. She doesn't like pubs any more, either."

"Well, you and I could slip out for a quick one. Just be about forty minutes." But she knew it was a brisk fifteen minutes' walk each way and they would hardly be content with ten minutes in the pub. Still, she wanted very much to go. She thought of the hedges they would pass. They were made up of rank wild greenery: alder and nettles and dock, and the prospect of plunging into the tunnelly lanes excited her. She had been abroad so long with Bandino that she felt the green English rural twilight would refresh her like a swim in lake water. Her father had always liked walking. They would stride quickly—because of getting back to her mother—bouncing on the ball of the foot along rubbery ground, not dusty as in Italy, nor concrete as in London, but ground that was responsive to the step. Like Antaeus, she would be restored. Then there would be the mild gleam of the pub. "Let's," she insisted.

"No," said her father. "Oh, I'm afraid", he giggled, "I've had too much already. Not used to it, you know. Feel tiddly."

So they returned to the living-room where her mother was watching the television.

"Look", said she, "at that"—it was a London fashion show—"I won't say 'indecency', because what is indecent nowadays, but at the sheer silliness of women over thirty wearing skirts that short!"

"They call them 'pussy pelmets'," said Priss, who had cautiously worn her longest skirt for this trip into the provinces. But she felt got at. She was sure her mother had guessed she was a trendy dresser.

"It's all right", her mother went on, "for teenagers. Rather sweet on *them*, in fact! I remember *you* had a sweet little kilt from the Scotch House when you were fifteen. Way above your knees, even though it wasn't the fashion then. That was 1956," she stated precisely. She looked back at the screen. "Now it suits *her*," she nodded approvingly at a pale waif in what looked like a plastic gymslip. "She must be about seventeen, wouldn't you say? Still boyish. It's these *old* things of thirty flattening down their breasts and wearing their hems above their bottoms that would make a cat laugh! How can they expect any man to take them seriously? They're neither children nor adults. Nothing."

"Oh, the men like it." Priss told her. "For the first time Englishmen are turning round in the street to look at women. Just like in France or Italy. The very first time. The décolletés never got them. They're leg men."

Her mother snorted. "They may *look*!" She said, "But do they *marry*?"

Oh, hell! Still trying to knock me sexually. Is she jealous *of* me or disappointed *for* me? If this is the way mother love curdles, it's a good thing I gave up Peregrine. Maybe it's because I didn't want to turn into a replica of *her* that I never married? Paul wouldn't have married me and Bandino won't, but Jeremy would have, like a shot, and that sweaty millionaire, and Michael, who is probably going to be a peer. God, the chances I've turned down. And I'm *nice* to men: patient and good-humoured and adaptable. There've been so many. I've *had* to be. And I'm not possessive or jealous at all! Whereas all she's ever been is spoiled and cosseted. A one-man-for-one-woman arrangement is inhuman. It should be stopped. She has him so utterly under her thumb!

He was fussing with his pipe.

"I think this new generation", her mother was saying, "is a great improvement on the last. The teens I mean. They're more imaginative."

"Well," said Priss, "people usually get on better with their grandchildren, don't they, than with their own children."

"I don't know what you're insinuating!"

"Nothing," said Priss. "Unless", it occurred to her, "that you're using the teeny-bopper generation as a stick to beat mine with."

"Who mentioned yours? You are touchy, I must say! How can you know what's going on in my mind?"

"Is it so obscure?"

"Don't be insolent," said her mother. "You're obviously loaded with complexes and the sense of failure. I'm sorry for you."

"Why do you provoke me like that?" Priss asked her.

"*Me* provoke you? Honestly! That's a good one." Her mother laughed theatrically. "Did you hear that, Edwin?" she appealed to Priss's father.

Puffing at his pipe, he gave no sign of having paid any attention to what had been said.

"I . . ." the mother began again.

"Oh, drop it, will you?" said Priss. "I've taken all I can take."

"You've taken all you can take!" shouted her mother. "Will you listen to that, Edwin, from your precious daughter? Will you? She can't set foot in this house, even after being away four years, without being offensive! It's intolerable. I don't ask what she's been doing. I'd rather not know. Although I've a good enough idea. And so have the neighbours. I can tell by the way they ask after her. And then getting you drunk and baiting me . . . yes, baiting! I can't stand it! I can't! From that—whore!" She began to sob violently.

Priss's father put down his tobacco pouch as though giving up a weapon. "Now, Roslyn," he patted his wife's shoulder, "pull yourself together. It's a little misunderstanding. That's all. She gets upset," he told Priss. "You must try not to upset her. It's those drugs she takes", he smiled vaguely, "for the diabetes." On the furry hearth rug, with the lamplight glinting on the hair of his hand, he looked furry himself: a domesticated animal.

"I think", said Priss, "I'll spend the night at the pub. I'll ring you in the morning. I'm sorry. No, I'm sure. Yes, I remember the taxi number. You stay here."

She telephoned a taxi from the hall, then went into the loo to comb her hair and put on lipstick. Her overnight bag was still by the front door where she had left it. It was uncompromisingly small. Had she ever meant to stay?

He came out to say good-bye. She must be sure to ring in the morning. "Mother will feel differently," he assured her. "She hasn't been quite herself. . . . Will you be all right alone?"

"Darling! In the English countryside? Of course! I'm a nightbird, you know!"

He took her out to the taxi and stuck his head through the window to kiss her good-bye. Then he withdrew it, bounced back up the porch steps, and flipped a hand along some hanging bamboo chimes in a gesture of spry farewell. Before the driver had managed to turn his vehicle in the narrow drive, the door had closed behind him and the hall light snapped on. Seconds later, Priss sighted his silhouette in the landing window turned away from her to engage in a pantomime of comic relief. With something much too large to be a handkerchief—a table-runner perhaps?—he sponged his brow and flung out his arms with the old clubman's vivacity. Suddenly her mother was in them and the two, floating like a bright icon above the dark doorway, remained clinging in a still, utterly relaxed embrace until Priss's taxi had made its noisy exit down their gravelled drive.